I0730351

NANIMA SERIES

Combined Volume 2: Books 3 to 4

SPIRITUAL FICTION

DONNA GODDARD

Copyright © 2025 by Donna Goddard

All rights reserved. No part of this book may be reproduced in any form or by any electronic or mechanical means, including information storage and retrieval systems, without written permission from the author, except for the use of brief quotations in a book review.

NANIMA SERIES: COMBINED VOLUME 2

BOOKS 3 TO 4

Sonder (Book 3)
The Flat (Book 4)

CONTENTS

SONDER

BOOK 3 OF THE NANIMA SERIES

PROLOGUE
DAWNING REALISATION

Sonder is the realisation that everyone has a story, and, for some people, you are merely a random passerby, an extra sipping coffee in the background.—The Dictionary of Obscure Sorrows by John Koenig

⬥

The increasing realisation that
every life and life form is as
intricate and marvellous as our own
is an indication of developing consciousness.

PART I
SOLSTICE
SUMMER

QI IS IN ME

CHAPTER 1

FIERY FATHER

December 22nd:

It was summer solstice and a few days before Christmas. The sun was at its highest, and the days were at their longest. The southern face of Earth was directly turned towards its source of power and light—its fiery father. The summer solstice is a time of maleness, a time for masculine qualities, which we should all have a balance of. It's a time for looking outward, being outside, speaking up, and generally doing stuff.

Being nestled in the ranges, the summer temperatures of Black Forest were considerably less than the lowlands. It was Maliyan's first summer in Black Forest, but she had already learned not to wrap summer in the concept of heat—instead to see it in terms of long days of light, relatively less clothing, and usually (but not always) unnecessary heating. It was a milder notion of summer. It meant you could go for an evening walk. It was a break from the long cold rather than a powerful hot season in its own right.

As Maliyan passed *Sonder,* the most popular cafe in town, she heard a woman say, "It's so beautiful out here that I would move too, but an eigth-month winter is too long for me."

"Nonsense. Who told you that? Winter isn't eight months," said

9

her male friend with a smile. "It's more like ten. And the other two, your house can burn down!"

Living next to a forest, everyone had to be fire-aware.

Someone had humorously decorated a large weed growing tenaciously through a crack of the dilapidated Municipal Council building next to Sonder. The baubles and tinsel merely drew attention to the building's unkempt state.

A woman descended the railway steps and clattered along the footpath with her suitcase. She probably caught the train out from the city to stay with her parents over the Christmas break. Her high heels were impractical for travelling. No doubt, she preferred city living to country comfort.

Maliyan walked through the miniature Christmas trees individually decorated by the local businesses. A sweet one had a hidden alcove amongst the branches with a tiny community of fairies and birds. All the businesses contributed, but there was a big discrepancy in tree-decorating talent. The worst one consisted of gum tree branches, which looked good for two days and then became a brown, dried-out structure of lifeless garden rubbish. A lone, silver tinsel star sat at the top, heavily leaning to one side. It didn't have a business name attached.

The unofficial but unanimous winner was an earthworks company that made a bright, sparkly tree with yellow toy trucks circling it, filled with red, green, and gold Christmas baubles. "Surprised they are still there," visitors would say as they pointed to the toy trucks. Not only did toy trucks stay in their rightful place, but cafe tables and chairs were left out overnight and were still there every morning. Safe to say, the crime rate was low.

CHAPTER 2

JIHUI AND ROBERT

Turning left, Maliyan stopped at a cottage in a side street. An A-board was placed on the sidewalk, saying:

FREE
Summer Solstice Empowerment
QiGong*
All welcome

A man at the entrance of the open shed smiled calmly and warmly. He gestured for Maliyan to come closer.

Bowing, he said, "My name is Robert. My Chinese name is Jihui." Seeing that Maliyan was engaged, he continued, "When my wife and I first came to Australia, the immigration officer asked me if I had an English name. I had forgotten to pick one, and Robert was the first name that popped into my mind. So, Robert, it has remained."

---

* Qi (pronounced che) means life force. QiGong is a traditional Taoist Chinese mind-body practice combining movement, breath, and meditation to improve balance, flexibility, strength, health, and energetic well-being.

He laughed quietly, and his eyes sparkled. His face was lineless, making it hard to tell how old he was, but his demeanour had the wisdom of age.

"Would you like to join us for qigong summer solstice empowerment?" asked Robert. "It's free—the session, summer solstice, and empowerment."

Entering the little shed, Maliyan sat on the floor with eight other people, all Chinese. She had a Chinese strain of DNA in her. Along with white settlers, they were the first non-Aboriginal people to come to Nanima. As a result, many Nanima families had some Chinese in them, although it was typically not acknowledged. She knew nothing about her paternal Chinese relative. A hairdresser once told Maliyan that she had Chinese hair because it sat so firmly in the direction it wanted to go. A local of Black Forest told Maliyan that her profile was identical to Penny Wong (a well-known Chinese-Australian politician). Wong was the first Asian Australian in Cabinet and the first openly lesbian federal parliamentarian in Australia.

"I hope you don't mind," he added tentatively.

"Of course not," said Maliyan. "She's one of the few politicians we trust, and she's a powerhouse."

CHAPTER 3

MR TANNER AND
MASTER XIAO

"**A**s we have some new people," said Robert [Maliyan was fairly sure that she was the only new person], "I will tell you a little of my story."

"I met my master, Master Xiao, when I was an eight-year-old boy in the early years of the Chinese Cultural Revolution, which began in 1966 and lasted for a disastrous decade."

Robert must be around sixty, thought Maliyan.

"Neither I, my family, nor the residents of our town knew that Master Xiao was a highly accomplished martial artist and qigong healer. We simply knew him as Mr Tanner, a gentle, quiet man who recently started working in the lowly job of boiler room attendant across the road from where we lived. I was sick with a mysterious illness that prevented me from attending school. When my parents were at work, I snuck out of the house out of boredom and began investigating everything I could get into. I soon came across the boiler room, and something about Mr Tanner's laughing eyes drew me into that hot space. I began calling in every day, and Mr Tanner asked me if I would like to learn martial arts from him. Of course, I said yes. However, I had to keep it a secret for everyone's safety.

I barely noticed that my health issue quickly disappeared. My training from Mr Tanner went on for many years. Eventually, my parents had to know. Along with my martial arts training, I began developing qigong energy abilities. After seven intense and marvellous years, a great shock came to me. The Cultural Revolution ended, and Mr Tanner had to return to the Buddhist monastery high in the remote mountains he came from. Mr Tanner was, in fact, Master Xiao, a widely respected and extraordinary monk at the temple. The monastery had been disbanded at the beginning of the Cultural Revolution, and all the monks had to return to their families. As Master Xiao was an orphan, he had no family to return to. Thus, he roamed the countryside for a few years before settling across the road from me.

After Master Xiao returned to his beloved Buddhist community, I continued my training with him. That meant many hours of travel during the school holidays by train and bus and then a five-hour trek up the mountain. My master did not want me to become a monk. He wanted me to be educated and travel to the West with the lineage."

Robert paused, looked at the clock, and said, "So, here I am. Let's begin."

After the summer solstice empowerment, which consisted of various qigong exercises, Robert said that they were going to see Master Xiao tomorrow, and everyone was welcome to attend.

CHAPTER 4

MEETING A MASTER

The next day:

It was an hour's drive to the mountain and then a two-hour trek to the top. Master Xiao was on an extended stay from China to celebrate his 94th birthday and would soon return to his own mountain. Maliyan decided to go with them because how often do you get to meet a master?

The mountain track was steep. Everyone seemed to be fitter than Maliyan. Maybe they were used to coming here to see Master Xiao. The little group stopped every half hour. If they were stopping for her, they didn't make it obvious. They said they were having a nature break, meditation break, or looking-at-the-view break.

Robert patiently walked beside her. He was an engaging storyteller and made the uphill trek considerably less tiring than it otherwise would have been. Along the way, she learned much about him, the master, and qigong. Maliyan concluded that underneath Robert's humble, relaxed, and unassuming manner was a powerful mind and significant spiritual accomplishment.

CHAPTER 5

SIX SOUNDS

The view from the top was spectacular. The simple temple and surrounding buildings took nothing from the mountain's glory. Everything seemed to be there to serve the cause of life in its magnificent, unadulterated beauty.

Master Xiao embodied effervescent happiness, peace, and ease. He was unexpectedly slight, given his still active physical abilities. Robert told Maliyan that when he first met his master, he was surprised that such a modest body could perform the feats that it did. He found it very amusing that if they walked in an unsafe area at night, his master's unimpressive build would appear as easy prey for robbers. He laughed heartily and said, "That was a grave mistake!"

As Master Xiao couldn't speak English, Robert translated the session.

"During the sixth century," said Master Xiao, "a QiGong master, who was nicknamed *Grand Councillor of the Mountains,* identified six sounds that have a unique healing effect on the human body. Each corresponds to a specific organ and energy system. Today, we will practise them."

The master explained the sounds, the relevant organs, and the order in which they would be chanted. They were:

1. Xu (pronounced shee) for liver
2. He (pronounced huh) for heart
3. Hu (pronounced hoo) for spleen
4. Si (pronounced suh) for lungs
5. Chui (pronounced chway) for kidneys
6. Xi (pronounced see) for the three centres or dantians

"The three dantians," said Master Xiao, "are the centres of qi or life force in our body."

The process was slowly taught over several hours. Then everyone ate a simple lunch. After that, the six healing sounds were practised reverently and profoundly. One of Maliyan's favourite bits was whenever Master Xiao said in Chinese, "I am in Qi. Qi is in me." There was something about how he said the words that radiated a powerful energy transfer. The words bristled with intensity and brightness.

At the end of the day, Master Xiao said,

"Many of the most magnificent things in our world happen gently, graciously, and with no fanfare—the movement of the sun, the stars, the moon, the ocean, and the constant miracles of creation in the natural world. You, too, can become a force of nature. Don't be afraid that your growth has to be painful and dramatic, involving lots of outward change. More often than not, it is a gentle unfolding of what is beautiful, true, purposeful and serene."

I am in Qi. Qi is in me.

PART II
LIVING IN FOG
WINTER

EVERYONE HAS A STORY

CHAPTER 6

AN EXTRA IN THE BACKGROUND

Six months later, in late June:

When the first month of winter is as cold as Black Forest, the long stretch ahead can seem rather daunting. The outside section of Sonder was empty, although inside was busy and buzzing as usual. The other cafes in town did alright, enough to get by, with the bonus of freedom. They would shut for all sorts of reasons—fire weather, winter break, baby born, spouse sick, no staff, mental health, changed our minds. Sonder, however, was different. The owners had run a thriving inner-city cafe and brought all their vibe and work ethic out to Black Forest when they decided on a lifestyle change for their young family. The couple were always pleasant to customers but a little reserved. Their focus was on running the business.

One day, Maliyan said to Ronny, one of the owners, "Did you name your cafe after the invented word?"

Ronny looked at her half-surprised, half-suspicious and said, "You know what it means?"

He waited for validation that she really did know the meaning of sonder.

"Ahh, something about..." said Maliyan, scrambling for a passable definition, "other people's lives being are as complex and real as our own."

"Yes," said Ronny, satisfied with her response. "Everyone has a story and, for some people, we are merely a random passerby, an extra sipping coffee in the background."

After a pause, he added, "You are only the second person to come in here who knows what the word means."

"Maybe others have known but didn't bother to say," said Maliyan.

Ronny's face suggested that he doubted that. From that moment on, they were friends.

CHAPTER 7

PASSERSBY

Luna pulled his beanie lower as he surveyed Sonder's vacant outdoor area. He had learned that when he drove out to Black Forest, he needed extra layers.

"Grand German shepherd," said a passerby, pointing to Iggy.

"Bit chilly," said Luna.

"Ahh, don't you mind that," said the man. "It's the cold and low-lying cloud (the dome, as we call it) that keeps them city folk from moving out here."

Luna tried to look less citified. He saw on his phone that it was winter solstice. It was a year since his first trip to Black Forest and six months since his move this way. As it turned out, he was living and working in the city and travelling the hour to Black Forest about once a month.

Maliyan kissed Luna hello, patted Iggy, and sat down.

A talkative couple exited Sonder and said, "Well-behaved dog. No lead. No nothing. No coat? You've got one."

"German shepherds have double coats," said Luna. "He's already got his winter coat on, and it's perfectly coordinated with his colouring."

CHAPTER 8

DOZEN A DAY

"Weak latte, I assume?" said Luna.

"No," said Maliyan, "I'm off caffeine. A few days after I saw you last, my body told me to get decaffeinated coffee in the mornings. So, I did. And a couple of days after that, it told me to get rid of the real drug."

"What drug?" asked Luna.

"Tea," said Maliyan. "One weak coffee a day was nothing compared to my tea intake. Country women of my generation are big tea drinkers. My sisters, female cousins, and I were all drinking tea by the time we were twelve. Lots of it. I probably drink a dozen cups of tea a day. Anyway, my body told me to drink decaffeinated tea instead."

"How did that go?" asked Luna.

"For a few days, I was falling asleep, and I felt depressed for no apparent reason. But then, my nervous system and whole digestive system got on board and started working much better than before."

Luna frowned and said, "It's *not* a real drug."

CHAPTER 9

SHROUDED IN MIST

"Except for a few short breaks," continued Luna with averted eyes, "I've always been a big weed user. Not public. It's been a private thing, which is probably worse."

Although Maliyan didn't know this about Luna, she was not surprised. A person of his sensitivities has to find some way of coping with life.

"You weren't using it when I was living in the shophouse a year and a half ago," said Maliyan.

"That was one of the short breaks," said Luna. "It's also why I deteriorated as the time went on. I wasn't ready to give it up." He looked uncomfortable but rallied himself and said, "When I moved down here, I knew that if I didn't get off it, I was going to create the same life all over again. And I wanted something better." Turning to the nearby mountain of Geboor, he could see that its summit was shrouded in mist. "So, yeah, I've been off it for six months. It's been really tough. It has affected me in many ways— eating, sleeping, what I do with my time. The worst side effects have been inability to sleep and brain fog. Thankfully, the fog is lifting now."

"So you decided to tell me," said Maliyan.

"Yeah," said Luna.

Maliyan leaned over the table, put her hand on Luna's shoulder, and said, "I've never been prouder of you."

THE LESSENING

LONGTIME LOVER

*O*ne month later, at Sonder:

Maliyan stared at Luna to see if there was any sign of him returning to his longtime love, Mr Marijuana.

"I'm still off it," said Luna with annoyance.

"Great," said Maliyan.

"Did you think I'd get back on it?" asked Luna.

Maliyan didn't want to say yes, but Luna had been quite changeable in the past.

"He's a hard lover to dump," shrugged Maliyan.

"I haven't gone through all this for nothing," said Luna emphatically.

Maliyan smiled approvingly at the unsmoked, defogged, cleaner, clearer version of Luna sitting beside her.

Two tradies waited outside Sonder for their takeaway. They leaned on the wall casually, their strong, bare legs seeming not to notice the bitter wind. Luna's seven months in the city had noticeably brought out his gayness. He was living and working in an area where he was not only free to express it, but encouraged to. He eyed off the ruggedly handsome men. He did it so openly and unashamedly that even though both men were probably straight, they took it as a compliment and laughed.

Maliyan, on the other hand, looked away. It wasn't that she was jealous or embarrassed. She didn't want to give any energy to Luna's highly flirtatious ways. He flirted with everyone—no one was left out. He wasn't a serious flirt. If anyone pursued the offer for more than ten seconds, he exited the scene. He had many chances to follow through with interested parties on both sides of the track and rarely took them up. This quality of non-neediness made his flirtations funny and endearing rather than unwanted.

Nevertheless, as Luna was becoming an unfogged being, Maliyan wanted him to keep going in that direction. If she laughed at his flirtations, it would have fueled the behaviour. If she looked even a minuscule jealous, it surely would have ignited it. The best approach seemed not to have an opinion about it. In that way, she was neither feeding nor resisting it, liking nor disliking it. We don't have to have an opinion about everything. And sometimes, the most helpful thing is not to.

CHAPTER 11

PRINCESS

"How's everything at your house? asked Luna.

"Bell-Bell's coming from Nanima in a few days," said Maliyan.

"That's nice," said Luna.

"Not really," said Maliyan.

Last spring, Bell-Bell decided not to sell her father's house and asked Maliyan to keep looking after it in exchange for cheap rent. She also wanted to visit Black Forest every few months. The visits were becoming less enjoyable for Maliyan, who had thought about alternative rentals, but nothing affordable was available.

"She's a princess," said Maliyan flatly.

"Well, yeah, that's obvious," said Luna. "What does her partner do about it?"

"Nothing," said Maliyan. "I guess he wanted a princess."

"If they are both happy..." said Luna.

"Who is happy with that?" said Maliyan. "If you are the master, you alternate between being satisfied with your servant and resenting that they are weak. If you are the servant, you alternate between being glad of having a god and resenting your lack of dignity. Not to mention, sex needs equals."

"You *did* mention it," said Luna.

"She can do better," said Maliyan.

"Better partner?" asked Luna.

"Partner is not the point," said Maliyan.

"Have you talked about it with her?" asked Luna.

"It goes very badly," said Maliyan. "Instead of being a straightforward princess, she turns into a psychological princess throwing justifications and veiled insults around left, right, and centre with her intelligent, offended brain."

"Then, don't do it," said Luna.

"That would be the end of the friendship," said Maliyan. "Anyway, I made a commitment to help her and I can't abandon that unless she makes it perfectly clear that she wishes it to be so."

"If you can't talk to her," said Luna, "it's not much of a friendship."

"Exactly," said Maliyan.

CHAPTER 12

TO A TEA

Early morning, a few days later:

"Got your chai on the way, lovely Maliyan," said Tim.

He and his brother, Tom, ran their Black Forest cafe, *To a Tea*, from their shop window. They had their operating system down to a tee. Tim was a bubbly, affable fellow who was great with all the different types of townsfolk who came his way. At forty, with a family of young kids, he was old enough to know the struggles of life but young enough to tolerate people's stupidity without complaint. He complained to his brother without restraint, but that was behind closed doors.

Tom stayed at the coffee machine. He didn't cope well with people, although, at home, he was happy enough. He kept his head down and focused on the more manageable coffee. There were some exceptions, and he walked the few steps from the coffee machine to the cafe window to deliver the coffee personally. Maliyan realised that he made this decision the first few times a new person came to the shop, and it rarely changed. On her second visit, he walked to the window and personally handed her order to her. Naturally, she would have taken no notice, but she saw that

Tim stopped working and smiled knowingly. After that, both men called her *lovely Maliyan* whenever she went to the shop.

DEAD WRONG

"I didn't get you a coffee," Maliyan said to Bell after returning home from To a Tea. "I thought you would still be doing your meditation practice."

"I'm better without it," said Bell, who had a highly reactive body.

Bell-Bell was reactive to many things, physical and mental. She said it was because of her neurodivergency. Maliyan tried to tell her that some issues had little to do with neurodiversity and much to do with the neurotypical functioning of the ego. However, it always resulted in some type of meltdown from Bell. Thus, the cycle continued, getting nowhere.

When it came to the few people Maliyan let into her inner circle, they could be any manner of thing on the outside, but inside, they had to have two clear orientations towards her. Firstly, they had to have a sincere, heartfelt love for her. It didn't have to be a perfect love by any stretch of the imagination, but it had to be the sort of love that if she weren't there anymore, they would suffer the loss deeply.

Secondly, they had to have an instinctive respect for her know-ingness about certain aspects of life. There were countless things

Maliyan didn't know, and in many areas, she was quite ignorant. But the essence of life, the nature of people, the evolution of individual consciousness—this she knew. If they couldn't see that or chose not to, competed with it, or belittled it, then she could not waste herself on them. They didn't have to understand anything about what Maliyan knew, but they had to trust it enough not to dismiss her efforts to help them. Maliyan didn't doubt that Bell fulfilled the first condition, but the second was dismantling before her eyes.

That evening, before retiring to bed, Bell said, "I know that you are trying to help, but the thing is, I know better than you about me."

It sounded so reasonable and said with the considered, educated tact of a psychologically sophisticated person. But both knew, it was dead wrong.

CHAPTER 14

AS FAR AS PARTNERS GO

T*he next day:*

"How's Luna?" asked Bell as Maliyan drove her to the airport for her return flight to Nanima.

"He's doing well," said Maliyan cautiously.

"Do you see him much?" asked Bell, trying to sound casual.

This was a no-win conversation. Nothing about it could help their flailing relationship. Although it was never spoken of, Maliyan had long sensed that Bell was interested in a couple relationship with her. Bell was like that. She had loose boundaries when it came to conventional living, which is one of the things Maliyan valued about her. However, Maliyan did not want that sort of relationship with her. Also, Bell had a perfectly good partner, as far as partners go. Regardless, changing partners wouldn't have helped.

If Maliyan had killed the idea earlier, there was a high chance that Bell would have aborted the whole relationship. Maliyan didn't want her to do that. Just because someone misunderstands how their path will unfold does not mean that they cannot, with time, accept and understand it. It takes perseverance and humility on the part of the path-taker and wisdom and timing on the part of the path-guide.

Bell was barking up the wrong tree for her evolution and happiness. There was something more valuable for her to gain than she could currently imagine. However, she first needed to transcend the fear and anger of her mental meltdowns. She needed to let down her years of carefully crafted defence. Would she be able to do that? Probably not. Not on her own. But last spring, she took a thread from Geboor—her thread. It was the thread that Francis spoke about in his Nanima poustinia.

> Everything is stored in
> the fabric of Geboor.
> Take a thread and
> pull it towards you.
> Not any thread.
> If you take the wrong one,
> it will fray away.
>
> Take the thread that is yours.
> Tie it around you.
> See how it remains anchored
> in the bowels of Geboor.
> Wind it around you so
> many times, you forget that
> once it was not a part of you.

At the time, Bell said, "The thread is much less *me* than I imagined it would be."

The *lessening* of Bell had begun and was now intensifying.

CHAPTER 15

WHEN EVERYONE IS GOOD

The twin-engine propellor plane taking Bell back home from Black Forest had ten passengers. With ten rows of three seats, everyone had a row to themselves. That was exactly as Bell and the other country passengers had anticipated. It was a little bumpy, as small planes tend to be, but stress-free and hugely quicker than an all-day drive.

The good-looking flight attendant served tea and snacks and asked each person how their day was going. His easy country smile was placid and generous. Whenever anyone asked him in return how his day was, he said happily, "I'm good when everyone else is good." He looked pleased with his philosophy, glad that as a rural lad of probably twenty-eight, he had come up with such a magnanimous approach to life. It genuinely did seem as if nothing much from inside him would ruffle him. Yet, somehow, his approach bothered Bell, who took it upon herself to educate him.

"That is a nice approach," said Bell, "but, you know, everyone has a right to their own feelings."

The host listened politely, thought for a moment, and said, "Would you like more tea or another biscuit?"

Bell decided to leave him alone.

The plane flew at a height of around 10,000 feet, well below the path of commercial jets. The winter countryside below was quite visible at that height and gave a delightful passing show of green hills and small towns. However, it didn't create much delight in Bell, although she felt it should.

CHAPTER 16

RING THE BELL

As the plane approached Thubbo airport, Bell's eyes traced the Wambul's watery course snaking through dreamland country. Once onboard the XPT to Nanima (the express passenger train), Bell again crossed paths with the river as it forged its way under railway bridges of clickity-clack metal and wood. The Wambul was moving in the opposite direction to her, having come from Nanima, where it had collected the Bell River.

The introduction of the rural XPT a few decades ago significantly improved travel time and comfort from Thubbo to the city, Nanima being its second stop. There was a choice of tickets—regular and first class. It seemed to Bell that there was no viable difference between a first-class and regular ticket. Nevertheless, she always spent a few extra dollars to get the first-class one. She had learned that, as one passenger put it, "First class gets rid of the riff-raff." Bell thought it was strange that for a few dollars, you could decide if you were worthy of the peace and quiet of a first-class ride or rough it a bit with the regular folk. First class was rarely full.

The train driver beeped at a lone roadworker on a nearby dirt track. The worker looked up and waved. Later, the driver blew his whistle at a farmer working his field on a tractor. Further on, he acknowledged a tradie on the roof of a dairy close to the railway track. The driver didn't whistle at groups of workers, only lone ones. Bell thought it was a way of saying, *Hey buddy, you are not alone. I see you.*

A woman sitting beside her started a conversation and commented that Bell-Bell was an unusual name.

"My real name is Laura-Bella," explained Bell, "but I was given the name Bell-Bell and tend to use it."

"You are in the right place with a name like that," said the woman.

"I guess so," said Bell.

Ignoring Bell's lack of enthusiasm, the woman continued, "I'm on my way to Nanima for Landcare Week. We are focusing on the Bell River erosion problems and launching a program called *Ring the Bell,* which will educate the farmers and townsfolk on how to best preserve the river."

"Perhaps it will help raise funds for the restoration of the low-lying bridge that got washed away in the flood two years ago," said Bell.

"Yes," said the woman, "but more important than the bridge is the river itself. We are destroying it. The collapse of the bridge is just a symptom. The junction of the Bell and Wambul Rivers is in crisis due to manmade erosion. People have pulled out the vegetation from the riverbanks, which has sped up the water. That, in turn, has meant the relentless cutting away of the rivers' banks and cliffs, and acres of topsoil have been washed away."

Listening to the woman's devoted and unselfish care for the land helped Bell to somewhat forget about her own problems.

"One of our educators did a little demonstration by putting an empty saucepan on a burning BBQ, and it quickly became hot," said the woman. "He then added water to the pot and explained how it slowed down the heating process. Lastly, he added some soil to slow the process down further. The moral of the story is that we need soil, trees, and healthy waterways, or not only will our manmade constructs be washed away, but we ourselves will ultimately perish."

THREE STRIKES

CHAPTER 17

DATE DAY

few days later, in Black Forest:

A It was a thrilling, sunny day—cold but glorious. A blue winter's day in Black Forest shines with brilliance against the backdrop of gloom. A week after Luna's last visit, he decided to drive out to Black Forest again and soak in the clear, smog-free sunshine. After their Sonder catch-up, they went for a creek walk. Iggy romped through the long, wet grass with the enthusiasm of a farm dog just let off his chain. Luna and Maliyan had nothing but happiness to share with each other. The spirited creek inspired more than usual depth in their conversation. All in all, a brilliant day.

TEXT MESSAGE FROM LUNA THAT EVENING

Hi boo. Had such a great day, I've decided I'll come out weekly from now on. It will be good for me.

MALIYAN

Great! I'd love that.

LUNA

It's a date then!

CHAPTER 18

CATCHING

The next week approached, and there was no message from Luna.

MALIYAN

Are we catching up?

No reply. If Luna didn't want to talk, he simply didn't answer. A lot of men do that.

NOT READY TO CONCEDE DEFEAT, MALIYAN TRIED AGAIN THE following day.

MALIYAN

Hi, love. Come out if you can. Iggy wants to be a country dog!

Nothing.

CHAPTER 19

FUEL FOR GROWTH

Although Luna was loved by many people for his widespread exuberance towards them, it wasn't by accident that he was still single. He was marvellous at intermittent relationships, not consistent ones. He said it was his parent's fault for modelling bad relationship behaviour. Maliyan didn't correct him because she was still in the stage of encouraging him to speak about things that he normally didn't speak about. However, one day, she would tell him, "If you grew up in a less-than-fortunate situation, then it needs to be turned into fuel for growth, not uncorrected bad behaviour."

Luna's inconsistency stemmed from his changeableness. Fluidity of thought can be a sign of an expansive mind, which is good. However, it can also be a sign of a fractured mind, which is not. If we want to get somewhere in life, we have to walk in a straight line (or, at least, a curving, back-and-forth one). We can't walk in circles, or we will never get anywhere. Luna tended to walk in circles. Maliyan trusted the core of Luna's heart, but outwardly, he could be irrationally and often insultingly contradictory.

The way he introduced her was a point in question. One day, when he was in a belittling frame of mind, he and Maliyan ran into someone outside Sonder. Luna introduced Maliyan as his "customer from Luna Tiks"! Sometimes, he introduced her as one of his besties. It could vary wildly. Maliyan suspected that the most complimentary he was of her was to other people, out of her earshot, to those she didn't know and would never know. Somehow, it would have seemed safer to Luna. Of course, it was a protective mechanism, but that did not lessen the destructiveness of the behaviour.

Earlier in the year, Maliyan had suggested that for the next get-together, they go to a nearby town, somewhere other than Sonder. Luna agreed. The day of the outing arrived. Maliyan was excited about the new adventure and messaged Luna before he left the city.

MALIYAN

Don't forget a coat in case the weather turns.

He didn't reply, but she assumed he was already on his way. When he arrived, he immediately headed into Sonder to order for them both. Realising that they were not going anywhere, and he hadn't even told her, Maliyan felt embarrassed and humiliated. Humiliation is a great silencer. It would have seemed pathetic to object, like a child waiting for a party invitation that never arrives. Isn't that how people are played, consciously or unconsciously? Take away the capacity for humiliation, and there is nothing left to play with. It may have been fear on Luna's part, but it was harmful and hurtful.

CHAPTER 20
BUSY BOO

The following week:

THREE STRIKES, HE'S OUT!

PART III
BECOMING
SPRING

CLOSED EYES

CHAPTER 21

WHERE RIVERS MEET

I n Nanima:

Luna's old cafe, Luna Tiks, had been bought and renovated by a local entrepreneurial family. The husband owned a real estate business, and the wife owned the cafe, now called *Where Rivers Meet*. It had a completely different feel to Luna Tiks— spacious, tastefully decorated with home decor items, and with a fire to add charm and warmth. The old shophouse that Luna had lived in was now part of the refurbished cafe. *Where Rivers Meet* was a hit with visitors and townsfolk. Even those who missed Luna had been mostly won over.

As Bell watched the steady spring rain through the cafe's clean window, a waitress approached and said, "Isn't it beautiful? I love it when it rains like this."

Bell mused that in Black Forest, the general response to yet another day of rain and greyness was commiseration. Here in Nanima, the rain was needed and appreciated, especially steady rain —consistent enough to soak deep into the earth but not manic enough to cause floods and wash away a year's income.

The waitress was a healthy, robust, twenty-year-old girl with no makeup and a fresh, straightforward face that looked like it would never be happier than jumping out of a Land Rover to open gates and rescue stray sheep. Something about the girl's uncomplicated happiness gave Bell an idea.

CHAPTER 22

RAIN ON ME

After walking to the junction of the Bell and Wambul, Bell followed the track upstream until she got to Euroka's hut.

"To what do I owe the pleasure of your company?" asked Euroka.

As his face was expressionless, Bell couldn't tell if he was making fun of her or complimenting her.

"Good to see you again," said Bell. "I was wondering if you had some spare time for me. I'm doing well, but..."

"If you are doing well, why do you need me?" asked Euroka.

Bell stiffened and said, "Will you help?"

Euroka turned his gaze to his beloved river and watched the rain make patterns on its skin.

"Come tomorrow morning at 6:00 a.m. for two hours," said Euroka, "and every morning after that for a week."

He didn't wait for a response but returned to his hut and left Bell alone in the rain.

CHAPTER 23

NO RESPONSE

When Bell arrived at Euroka's the following morning, he indicated for her to sit cross-legged under a gum tree next to the river.

"Two hours," he commanded. "Don't get up. Don't close your eyes. If I see them closed, that's the end."

"Don't close my eyes?" protested Bell.

"Last warning—don't speak either," said Euroka, closing his hut door.

Luckily, Bell had a naturally flexible body and could sit cross-legged without undue stress. Not closing her eyes was more problematic. She had to admit that she did have a tendency to fall asleep or daydream when her eyes were closed.

The first hour was spent ranting in her head about Euroka:

- Isn't he grateful that I came to him?
- Doesn't he realise that I am an advanced spiritual student?
- Why does he have to be so condescending?
- Maybe it was a mistake to come here.
- It was definitely a mistake.
- It's not like he is inundated with people asking for his help.
- I'll show him!

After an hour, Euroka appeared. Bell had momentarily closed her eyes (maybe more than a moment), but his noise jolted them open. He potted around his vegetable patch, appearing to take no notice of her, and then went back inside. It started raining.

Another hour to go, thought Bell. *And I'm getting wet. And I feel worse than before I started. I think I'll leave and not even tell him.*

A kookaburra laughed in a branch high above her. It stopped Bell's train of thought. She looked at the river, which seemed elated with the wet weather. Recalling the thread she pulled from Geboor, a subtle sense of acceptance entered her body. It was like a distant ship, so far away that one questions its existence. Bell tried to pull it closer, but it disappeared over the horizon, and she returned to her former mental state. Not exactly the same. She was a touch more settled. Partially accepting that she was going to be wet, uncomfortable, and couldn't close her eyes, the next hour passed slowly but surely. When the time was up, she stood, stretched, and knocked on Euroka's door. No response.

CHAPTER 24

OPEN EYES

Every morning at 6:00 am, Bell returned to the river, although all but the last morning were touch and go as to whether she would turn up or not. On the final day, although nothing had changed and Euroka was as unengaged as at the beginning, she felt calm as she sat cross-legged, open-eyed, watching the river, and being quite prepared that she would end up wet again. The rain was in no hurry to leave.

"If you wish, you may close your eyes today," said Euroka.

Although Bell had been dying to close her eyes all week (maybe as an escape, maybe in the hope of finding relief or being blessed), now that she was allowed to, she was not especially driven to do so. When she did close them, she found it wasn't particularly different from having them open. Or was it the other way around—that eyes open wasn't different to eyes closed? Either way, she knew it was progress.

"You may feel that I'm harsh on you," said Euroka at the end of the session. "Take it as a compliment. I do not waste my time and energy."

Bell couldn't help but glow inside. One such comment from Euroka was worth fourteen hours of sitting in the rain rudderless.

"When you think you're going well," said Euroka, "you're generally going poorly. And when you feel deflated, you're often much closer to making progress. You have created such a thick defence that it has become your greatest enemy. It is all one big, stupid, unnecessary lump of fear. Don't you see how the river watches over you? Don't you hear how the kookaburra keeps you amused? Once you learn that your fear is entirely unnecessary, your potential will blossom."

Ever since Euroka returned from Uluru two years ago, certain things about him had changed inexplicably. For one thing, his style of speech was more eloquent and sophisticated, as if he had undergone a whole system of education while away (although that was not possible because he had only been gone for a few months).

Maybe he downloaded it at Uluru, Bell thought.

She was about to say she could already feel her potential blossoming, but Euroka continued. "When you sit with the river long enough—not sleeping, not making things up, just sitting, just being—there is a chance of becoming, a chance of becoming something more until, one day, you become the river."

HOME AWAY FROM HOME

CHAPTER 25

DREAM HOME

Maliyan couldn't remember if the strangely familiar place first became known to her in a dream or a meditation. It didn't matter because some dreams are meditative, and some meditations are dreamy. The place was becoming more familiar with repeat appearances. It was home, a different home to Earth, a place of belonging. As far as Maliyan knew, it didn't have a name. It was not necessary. Things were known by a nameless sort of energy. The places and people there were recognised by their unique energy combinations.

The dream-meditation always began in the same way, with a distant song that was profoundly known, yet Maliyan could never quite put her finger on the tune or the lyrics. It was singing of something she knew to be precious, but if she concentrated, it would fade and become inaudible.

The planet was similar to Earth but with more variety of life-forms and greater intensity. Intensity of what? Colour, energy, ability to create. In their physical form, most people loosely resembled humans, which suited the planet in the same way humans suit Earth. However, unlike humans, a lot of time was spent in their

67

invisible energy bodies. There was a great variety of physical forms, which added to the fun of the place.

CHAPTER 26

FAMILY

And there was family. Maliyan's "parents" were parents to many. They were very tall, whitish, and extremely benevolent. She felt highly protected and nurtured in their presence, as did everyone. Most people lived alone, although no one ever felt lonely because the entire population was highly connected. If they wanted to talk to someone, all they had to do was think of them, and the conversation began. It began even if the other person was otherwise occupied because they could all manage numerous realities simultaneously.

The planet's inhabitants lived in homes made from natural substances readily available in the environment, such as wood, grass, and mud. The houses merged into the landscape unobtrusively and seemed to disappear when not needed. No one lived in big houses with empty rooms. Everyone's house was exactly the size they needed, so not too much time was spent looking after them.

Each person also cared for their surrounding land, usually a few acres. Food was cultivated on the acreage. It was perfectly aligned with the resident's needs. The longer they lived there, the more in sync the food became. They also had herb patches for medicines when needed. Anything else required was ordered from small local depots, which were every ten kilometres. There were no cities or towns. There were no cars as the residents all walked or sometimes teleported. There was no pollution. There was also no type of predatory nature, even amongst the animals. Nature was in perfect balance.

The population of the planet was significantly less than Earth's at about one billion. It was kept steady at that size, although no one was forbidden to reproduce. Residents could volunteer for the assignment. Generally, those with the desire to reproduce had excellent DNA and outstanding nurturing qualities. In the bulk of people, the desire for sex and reproduction was largely dormant, although it could be activated if one chose. Usually, it was left unactivated so that energy was channelled into other areas of life. No more than one offspring came from one family grouping. Parenting was a mutual and karmic decision to dedicate twenty years of their existence to child-raising. Regardless, the two tall beings were still known to everyone as ultimate parents, and their DNA was in all beings on the planet. So, in that sense, they truly were everyone's parents.

CHAPTER 27

TENANTS

One of the planet's primary functions was to help less developed planets in other galaxies. Earth was definitely considered underdeveloped and in dire need of assistance. Half the population of the dream planet (half being 500 million) spent a substantial part of their lifespan (a lifespan was generally 200 years) dedicating themselves to the growth of other planets. As so many residents had "jobs" requiring them to travel to other galaxies, the planet seemed to have a much lower population than it actually had. When Maliyan was there, she was aware that Earth was an impossibly long way away by human standards, but the inhabitants of the dream planet had far superior forms of transport to Earth and found the distance no problem or barrier.

Everyone on the planet had long ago learned to live peacefully, intelligently, and lovingly. Although there were different opinions, no one ever fought. Ever. Also, the concept of ownership didn't exist. Everyone was a tenant—of property and even more so of relationships. This entirely removed the demands, frictions, jealousies, disappointments, tyrannies, and endless problems that Earth people usually experience. It meant that the dream planet inhabitants had an innate honesty in their communications. There was nothing to hide because each person's path was respected and trusted, including one's own.

❧

WHEN MALIYAN WOKE ONE MORNING AFTER VISITING HER dream home, she recalled an Earth interview with movie star Nicole Kidman shortly after separating from her famous husband, Tom Cruise. Kidman said that although they had houses all over the world, not one of them felt like home. The comment always stayed in Maliyan's mind as a reminder that a home has nothing to do with a house. Houses cost money. Homes cost your spirit. Some homes, such as Maliyan's dream home, cost the recollection of your boundless and multidimensional nature.

TYE AND BYE

CHAPTER 28

BYE

In *Black Forest:*

Ronny, the co-owner of Sonder, looked at Maliyan oddly from his post behind the coffee machine. When it was her turn to order, he left his post and told the waitress that he'd do this one.

"I'm not sick," said Maliyan, pointing to her face mask.

Ronny shrugged to reassure her that it was fine.

"I've been to Dr Tye in The Flat," said Maliyan.

"Respected by many people," said Ronny, "including me."

"I had to have a spot removed from my face, so I'm covering it with this mask," explained Maliyan.

"You still look beautiful," said Ronny in a totally uncharacteristic way for his standoffish manner.

He then walked back to the coffee machine and let the girl take everyone else's orders.

It was not until the following week that Maliyan could

make sense of Ronny's curious behaviour. Sonder had new owners. It was his goodbye.

CHAPTER 29

DR TYE

In The Flat:

The Flat was the next town citybound to Black Forest. It was presumably named after the river flats on which the town was built. Unlike the dense tree population of Black Forest, The Flat was a rolling green valley. In Black Forest, the trees lived so close to you that you could hear them breathing. In The Flat, you could see the ever-changing expanse of sky.

When Maliyan returned to The Flat to get her stitches out, Dr Tye was his normal attentive self.

"How are you?" he asked, entering the room.

THE FIRST THING MALIYAN HAD NOTICED ABOUT DR TYE WAS the way he said, *"How are you?"* Many people ask the question without even looking at you, let alone waiting for an answer. Dr Tye not only looked at you but waited for a response and then listened to what you said. It was such an unusual trait that when he first did it, Maliyan didn't respond. She was used to thinking, *Why waste your breath responding to questions that people have no interest in knowing the answer to?* After an awkward silence, she realised that Dr Tye was waiting. "Oh, ahh, good," she spluttered. "Yes, good. Thanks!"

❧

BACK TO TODAY:

"I'm going well," replied Maliyan. "Thanks for asking. And you?"

"Let's get those stitches out," said Dr Tye as he reached for his scissors.

Although he attentively listened to other people's problems, he didn't burden his patients with his own.

CHAPTER 30

ROLE REVERSAL

In *To a Tea:*

Maliyan's morning cafe stops alternated between Sonder and To a Tea. She wanted to support both and enjoyed the different ambiance of each. Sonder, being a transplant of a city cafe, had upmarket, trendy attention to detail. However, the true-blue, country-bloke nature of the two To a Tea brothers (who knew everything and everyone of local interest) had a simple charm that held equal value.

Recently, the To a Tea brothers had made a small indoor seating area. As they were trying to coax customers out of their window ordering habit, Maliyan had taken to sitting indoors. Sometimes, she was the only one sitting there. As she was making no noise, the brothers would forget she was there and start speaking amongst themselves in their brotherly banter—more swearing, more complaining, and a surprising role reversal. At the window, Tim (the younger brother) was the frontman, the protector, the voice. In private, Tom upheld his older brother status as steadier, reassurer, confidant, and guide.

"Bye, boys," said Maliyan on her way out.

79

"Oh, bye, lovely Maliyan," said Tim. "Apologies for the language. We forgot you were there."

CHAPTER 31

STAYING ALIVE

In Sonder:

Someone who definitely preferred the upmarket trendiness of Sonder was a woman Maliyan later came to know as Leteisha—well-mannered, quick to compliment, dressed with tasteful money, educated, and entirely pleasant. The reason she caught Maliyan's eye was because an interesting story was unfolding.

Maliyan initially noticed the effort Leteisha put into thanking the cafe staff and smiling at people she knew and even those she didn't (including Maliyan). However, there was an underlying nervousness, bordering on anxiety, that lay below the surface. Maliyan also noticed that Leteisha had a wedding ring, but she had never seen a husband with her. Leteisha was the sort of person who could easily attract a great partner and also the sort of person to need one.

Then, a man started sitting with her. He was about her age (fiftyish), confident, relaxed, and at ease with the world. As the weeks and months passed, it went from an occasional catch-up to a daily occurrence. The man certainly wasn't Leteisha's husband. They were too wide-eyed engaged. There was too much excitement between them. They were also careful, like when you walk at breaking dawn and can't clearly see the ground ahead. Not a husband. Nor a friend—friends aren't *that* exciting.

Leteisha was obviously falling in love with the man (obvious to Maliyan, perhaps not to all the other table occupants in Sonder). At first, it was tentative and guarded. Then, throwing the good sense of fifty years into the wind, it was an exuberant fall into falling in love. Fortunately, the man also seemed to share the feeling, even if a little less...

What is it less of? wondered Maliyan. *Desperate. Desperate? That's weird. Leteisha is not a desperate woman. So, why does something feel desperate?*

Soon after, Maliyan was told by a local that Leteisha's only son, a young man of twenty, had been killed in a car accident. She also found out that Leteisha's husband was Dr Tye! Beautiful Dr Tye.

Oh no, thought Maliyan. *Poor Dr Tye. He lost his son and now his wife. And maybe he doesn't even know he has lost his wife.*

Maliyan did not blame Leteisha. She and Dr Tye would have had a marriage as wonderful and successful as they both were. But when a child dies, a mother has to find a reason to...stay alive.

I COULD SEE PEACE

CHAPTER 32

NEITHER GOOD NOR BAD

In Black Forest:

It had been several months since their last Sonder rendezvous. When Maliyan saw Luna, any thought of him playing her went out the window. From the expression on his face and the feel of his energy, the only person he had been playing was himself. And he wasn't enjoying it.

"If you could see me the way I see myself," sighed Luna, "you wouldn't like me. I suppose you only see yourself as a good person."

"I don't see myself as a person at all," said Maliyan.

"I didn't have the heart to tell you," said Luna, "but I got back on the weed."

"And Dr Tye?" asked Maliyan.

"He's helping me with some sleeping pills while I get off it again," said Luna. "The doctor I went to in the city was a d***head and said I'd get addicted to the sleeping pills just like I was to the marijuana. I felt worse than when I walked into his office, and that was pretty damn bad. It's all just so f***ing hard."

He put his head in his hands.

After an extended silence, Maliyan said, "Let's go for a walk."

They quietly talked about things of no particular consequence as they followed the creek's winding course. And with each watery bend, the struggle dissipated into the clean air of the breathing trees.

CHAPTER 33

ALL CONCERNED

"Hello, darling," said Bell as Maliyan answered the phone. "How are you?"

"Great to hear from you," said Maliyan. "I was wondering how things were going for you back in Nanima."

It was a few months since Bell's last visit to Black Forest.

"I know I can be honest with you," said Bell.

That's a good start, thought Maliyan.

"When I got back home, I felt terrible," said Bell. "Then, in the first week of spring, still feeling terrible, I went down to Euroka, and he gave me a retreat program. Really, it was just sitting by the Bell. I'm not so ignorant as to not realise that sitting in the presence of someone like Euroka (particularly since his Uluru journey) can impact a person greatly."

"And did it?" asked Maliyan.

"At first, I thought it didn't help me much, which was disappointing. But then I noticed that the tide had turned. More than just turning around, certain things in my mind became clear to me in a way I had never been able to grasp before."

"What were they?" asked Maliyan with genuine excitement.

"It was more of a losing something than gaining something," said Bell. "It was a lessening rather than an increasing, but, oh, how much better I feel."

"That's wonderful," said Maliyan.

"The day after my retreat," said Bell, "I was walking along the Bell River to the shops, and a thought came to me. It has stayed with me ever since."

"What was it?" asked Maliyan.

"***I could see peace instead of what I see right now,***" said Bell. "It seems simple, doesn't it? Such a little thing. Swap the complaint, anger, and fear thought for a peaceful one that isn't complaining, isn't angry, and isn't afraid. Simple, but, by God, not easy. It was only because I felt so bad that I gave it a real shot."

"That's beautiful," said Maliyan.

"The whole thing made me feel significantly more settled. I didn't have to be right or wrong about anything. It was irrelevant. I didn't have to work out what to do. And I stopped thinking about my relationship. I don't mean that in a bad way, but I stopped endlessly ruminating about it. What a relief. *Everything* has been going so much better, and I've had many creative ideas. I must have made some space for them."

After a long pause, Bell said, "Enough of me! How are you?"

"Going well, love," said Maliyan. "The weather has greatly improved. Spring has been divine. When are you visiting next?"

"That brings me to my next point," said Bell. "You know how I was going to sell my father's house last spring but changed my mind after visiting Geboor and pulling my thread from the mountain?"

"Yes," said Maliyan.

"Now that my mind is clearer and I am calmer," said Bell, "I have decided to sell my father's house after all, which means, of course, that you will have to move. I'd like it sold by summer, if possible."

"Not long then," said Maliyan.

"I shouldn't say I *decided* to sell my father's house," said Bell. "It was one of the ideas that became obvious of its own accord."

"In that case," said Maliyan, "it will be the right idea—for you, for me, and for all concerned."

PART IV
THE FLAT
SUMMER AGAIN

GUIDING LIGHT

CHAPTER 34

FROM ABOVE

It was 4 a.m. and Maliyan was driving from Black Forest to The Flat. The car was so full that she couldn't see out the back window, but it didn't matter because no one else was on the road. The sky was clear, and the stars were in all their glory. Luna sometimes said that the middle-of-the-night stars were the best because you didn't have to share them with anyone else. Maliyan thought that the stars were like love. They don't diminish with shining.

Bell sold her father's house, and in perfect synchronicity, the right one appeared in The Flat for Maliyan. It had a paddock at the back of the house that reached the creek below. The house was at one of the town's entrances, but being a country town, the shops were still very walkable.

As Maliyan had woken at 3:30 a.m. (wide awake), she thought it best to get up and start transporting her belongings because it was moving day. When she pulled up at her new rental, the stars seemed to glow even more brightly. They were such good company and so reassuring. How could one ever feel alone with that much tender light from above guiding the way?

CHAPTER 35

FOOLPROOF

> I've decided to move back up north. I gave it a shot. It's not working down here. Love you. x

There is a guiding principle in life that tells us to follow our loves. What are our loves? Anything that creates a passion, a fire, an instinctive interest in us. Follow it. When you have choices before you, follow the one that creates the most amount of enthusiasm in you. If it is a tiny fire, still follow it. Passion is your creator's way of letting you know which way to go. It is foolproof. Follow it wholeheartedly and use everything you have to make it work.

However, there is another guiding principle of equal importance. If you reach a brick wall, don't bang your head on it. You will only hurt yourself. The longer you keep banging, the more blood there will be. It is there for a reason. The road ahead wasn't going to work. Wipe the blood away, dust yourself down, dry your tears, and take a moment to assimilate your loss. Then, turn in a different direction and keep moving. Up ahead, unbeknown to you, is a clear road waiting for your footsteps.

Use both of these guiding principles—follow your passion but don't insist on the outcome—and your path will lead around all the obstacles and bring you to majestic vistas.

⁂

MALIYAN

> Alright.

LUNA

> Please don't think it's you. It's not. It's me.

MALIYAN

> There's no question of who it is.

SILENCE.

MALIYAN

> The thing is, Luna, you make me nervous. You do and say so many thinly-covered, dismissive and insulting things that I have to prepare myself to get hurt. I know that's not the kind of relationship you want with me, but that's what's happening. So, it's better you go than do things you regret. Safe travels, and I love you, too.

SYNCHRONISTIC SIGNS

CHAPTER 36

HAPPY BIRTHDAY

In The Flat:

As Maliyan entered the cake shop, Dr Tye held the door open and said, "Hi, Maliyan, nice to see you."

"Someone's birthday?" asked Maliyan, pointing to the cake with *Happy Birthday* written on the top.

"Yes," said Dr Tye.

He was about to leave but stepped back inside and moved away from the door traffic. His eyes were downcast.

"It's my son's birthday," he said. "He died a few years ago."

He then looked at Maliyan piercingly with the unlikely hope she may have some magic way of lessening the pain. Maliyan met his gaze, which was as pain-drenched as any gaze could be. She didn't move, didn't flinch, didn't say anything. Some things cannot be carried by words, but to know that another human is not afraid to see our pain—as it is, in its raw, ridiculous horror—somehow makes it more bearable.

"I still don't have words..." said Dr Tye.

Maliyan nodded.

The moment of torture softened its grip, and Dr Tye went to

the counter and asked for a knife. He cut a large piece of cake and handed it to Maliyan in a serviette.

"Are you sure?" asked Maliyan politely.

Dr Tye nodded and said, "There's only me to eat it."

CHAPTER 37

DROP THE DOCTOR

Over the next few days, Maliyan ran into Dr Tye three times: once at the cafe, once at the supermarket, and once at the bank.

"Three times lucky," said Dr Tye as he pulled his cash from the automatic teller.

"Hello again, Dr Tye," said Maliyan.

"Please, drop the doctor. It's Tye."

Maliyan smiled.

After a quick chat, he said, "I'm going to the new Thai restaurant tonight. Would you like to try it, too?"

"I don't really eat at night..." said Maliyan. "But, sure, why not?"

◆

At the end of a delicious and relaxed dinner, Tye walked Maliyan to her car and said, "Thank you. I enjoyed that. Maybe we could do it again?"

Maliyan thought for a moment and said, "Could I please say something?"

"Of course," said Tye maturely.

103

"If you want a friend, I could be that. If you want a close friend, I could probably be that too, but I'm not girlfriend or partner material."

Tye was an intelligent and considerate man, but he was also a fairly conventional one, at least compared to Maliyan. She knew she was pushing the boundaries of what he could cope with by having this conversation, but she felt it was worse to put him in a position where he could be hurt. Besides, if he actually did want to be friends, he had to show that he was willing to meet some amount of mental challenge without immediately bailing.

"You could easily find a lovely woman," continued Maliyan. "Good company, someone to care about you, share stories with and talk to about your day. Maybe even someone to share more than that if it worked out that way. I'm not that person. I'm more monk than anything else. I only look normal on the outside."

Tye made a face as if to say, *Do you look normal?* Both laughed, breaking the awkwardness of the conversation. See what a good man he was? He knew how to make the conversation easier and cared enough to do so. Nevertheless, he got the point, and Maliyan felt relieved.

Although Maliyan understood Tye's desire to re-partner, which would be exacerbated by seeing his wife in love with someone else, she felt he was capable of more. Would re-partnering fix his problems? Would it take away his pain? Would it guarantee him personal happiness? At the beginning, maybe. But for how long?

There is nothing intrinsically wrong with seeking a couple relationship. It fulfils many needs, but the concept of a romantic relationship as the highest pinnacle of life, worthy of all the hype, is faulty. And once in it, most people become so focused on its maintenance that it monopolises their attention for the rest of their life. If Tye resisted the urge to run after it and turned inwards to investigate the essence of his own life, then his rewards would be disproportionally great. Later, after he found his way in new territory, if he wanted someone, then he wouldn't even have to look. They would find him.

For some people, entering a couple relationship will give them the most impactful lessons for their individual growth. Some need to learn how to manifest a well-functioning, beneficial relationship. Some simply need the benefits of a relationship. Other people need to develop their aloneness and focus on their internal progress. It depends on what people need the most at their particular stage of development, and it also depends on karmic timing. All situations have their joys and challenges, and all can be used for our growth. What is best and when it is best requires intuition, trust, and courage.

"Let's see if we keep randomly bumping into each other," said Tye lightheartedly. "If we do, we'll take it as a sign."

BACK TO OUR ROOTS

CHAPTER 38

MELT

"You don't sound so good," said Maliyan, answering the phone.

"No, I'm not," said Bell. "I've been sick for a week and can't shake it. My head is in a lot of pain. Can you do something?"

"Yes," said Maliyan. "Are you somewhere you can lie down? Can you put the phone on speaker without anyone else hearing?"

"I'm at home," said Bell. "I'll close the bedroom door."

"Lie down, close your eyes, and breathe in," said Maliyan calmly. "Hold your breath. Breathe out. Do this again three times slowly.

Rest your arms beside your body, palms facing down. Breathe in and then pat the bed several times with your palms as you breathe out. Repeat two more times.

Turn your palms to face upward. Put your attention on your

right palm and feel a ball of energy in it. The energy ball is growing to a couple of inches. Keep your attention there for about thirty seconds.

Move your attention to your left palm and feel a ball of energy in it. Feel the energy growing. Keep your attention there for about thirty seconds.

Move your attention to your third eye, the middle of your forehead, between your eyebrows. Feel that my thumb is pressing lightly on your third eye. It is slowly, very slowly, opening. You can see a tiny ball of light growing to a few inches.

Focus your attention on your right palm again, then on your left palm, and then on your third eye. You're making a triangle. Do it again: right palm, left palm, third eye. Keep going for thirty seconds.

This time, as you do it, move the triangle out to one foot from your body. Right palm, one foot out. Left palm, one foot out. Third eye, one foot out. Trace the triangle in your mind—right palm, left palm, third eye, one foot out from your body.

Push the triangle out to ten feet from your body. Ten feet from your right palm. Ten feet from your left palm. Ten feet from your third eye. You are making a large triangle of energy, and you are in the middle of it. It's a temple. You are the centrepoint of the temple. You are utterly, entirely safe.

Push the triangle out to one hundred feet from your body. One hundred feet from your right palm. One hundred feet from your left palm. One hundred feet from your third eye.

It's a large, energetic triangle. All of it is safe. It is energised. You are in the middle of it.

In this safe space, your body and mind expand. Your feet melt into the bed. Your calves melt into the bed. Your thighs melt. Your stomach, hips, and buttocks melt. Your chest, back, and shoulders melt into the bed, to the floor, through the Earth, and into the ether. Your neck melts, and your head becomes lighter and lighter.

Put your attention on your jaw and invite it to relax. Focus on your thyroid at the bottom and front of your neck. It's like a butterfly. It spreads its wings and becomes lighter.

Feel my finger on your left temple. All the muscles and cells in your left temple are relaxing. Then, feel my finger on your right temple. All the muscles and cells in your right temple are relaxing.

In this sacred temple, crystal water runs through the entire space. It runs through you. The cleansing water enters your third eye, moves to the left temple and clears away the blockages and stuck points on the left side of your face. It now moves to your right temple, clearing away all the blockages. The healing water is running behind the back of your eyes, making your eyes feel clean and light.

The crystal water moves to the top of your head, to your crown, forming a ball of energy, and then moves itself in a swirling circle. It moves a foot above your head and makes an infinity sign (a figure eight on its side).

Now, it comes back to your crown and slowly, very slowly, like honey, starts running down the back of your head. As it travels down, it relaxes every muscle and every cell. It gets to the base of your head, where your skull meets your neck, and stays there. It forms a round ball and moves around, clearing the energy.

Your body is completely relaxed. There is space inside. Your mind has expanded into the one hundred feet of the sacred temple. Your body has become loose and light, and your mind has become spacious and translucent."

CHAPTER 39

RETURN OF THE DREAM HOME

Maliyan then took Bell to a new, ever-so-old place.

"We are now going to a faraway place," continued Maliyan. "It's *very* far away, but we'll get there instantly. You'll recognise it as another home, more of a home than where you are now on Earth. You are delighted to be there amongst the majestic trees. The atmosphere pulses with invigorating aliveness. You're standing outside your home, which looks similar to everyone else's home, green and natural-looking. It's a simple home, but it has everything you need. It feels incredibly comforting.

One of the planet's Wise Ones is there to greet you and says, *'Going to Earth is a tumultuous experience, and you must be careful not to start disintegrating like Earth people do. You are safe and can have a pain-free existence. Although you will experience Earth emotions, you do not have to take them into your body, mind, and energy field.'*

Walk into your garden and see the delightful flowers and healthy, abundant food that is specifically synced with you. Sit cross-legged on the soil. It feels warm, soft, and damp. Take your right hand and make a hole in the soil. Touch the roots. Underneath everyone's plot of land is an extensive, complex, intelligent root system. This system not only keeps each home's garden alive but is connected to each person's energy field. The root system keeps the home occupier functioning in a vibrant, energised form. Now, dig into the soil with your left hand. Dig deeper so that you have more contact with the roots. The root system transfers its healing energy to you. It feels balanced and harmonious. It removes the waste products from your energy field.

The Wise One tells you it is time to return to Earth. They take hold of your hand and pull you towards them. As an energetic being, the Wise One can take any physical form they want. They put your head on their chest and cradle it.

'You are well,' says the Wise One, reassuringly. *'When you go back to Earth, take your true essence with you. Your light does more than you realise. It is helping to elevate the planet's collective consciousness so that Earth-dwellers become a more advanced civilisation of beings.'*

Return to your Earth-body. You are pain-free and happy. Feel the creative fire inside you. Know that any negative experience is temporary and can be healed by remembering who you are. The vast energy system cleans and helps you. It reminds you of your immense connectedness with the Universe."

WISE WORDS

CHAPTER 40

SMALL DEATH, BIG LIFE

The next day, in Black Forest:

As Maliyan weaved her way through the miniature Christmas trees of Black Forest, she pulled a leafy twig from a gum tree and used it to brush away the flies. It was the common bushman's fly-fan.

Turning left, she stopped at Robert's cottage in the side street. She hadn't seen him since last summer solstice. Apparently, not long after Maliyan met Master Xiao, the master returned to China and died a week later. Robert and his wife immediately left for the monastery in the remote mountains of Hunan province. Maliyan assumed they had been there all year because every time she passed the cottage, it looked locked and lifeless.

At that moment, Robert walked out with an A-board.

FREE
Summer Solstice Empowerment
QiGong
All welcome

When he saw Maliyan, he put the board down, bowed, and smiled warmly.

"You're back!" said Maliyan.

"Just back," said Robert. "I thought I better remind people that summer solstice is coming up."

"How was everything in the mountain monastery?" asked Maliyan.

"At the beginning of the year, the morning of Chinese New Year, Master was found on his bed, sitting in lotus position, with a smile and eyes closed," said Robert. "He was dead. By the time we got there, he had already been gone for four days, but his body didn't smell. It didn't smell for the whole week leading up to the traditional barrel burial. Although most people are cremated so they do not hang around their bodies, enlightened people can be buried because they know what they are doing when it comes to death."

Someone in a passing car honked their horn and waved at Robert, who waved back.

"We then helped the ten remaining monks with the monastery," continued Robert. "They are all in their eighties and consider me a youngster. They couldn't cope with the workload of the monastery, so my wife and I arranged for tradespeople to come. We also tended to their personal needs. It took six months to sort out the monastery and aged care visits. At that point, my wife left to visit family, and I stayed behind to redo a one-hundred-day fast."

"One hundred days?!" said Maliyan.

"Yes," said Robert. "When I was fifteen, I visited Master Xiao in his mountain monastery and expected a wonderful summer holiday. After a few days, Master told me I was ready for Biguan practice, a one-hundred-day fast in a dark stone chamber. It's obviously a very demanding practice, but Master was never wrong about such things.

The chamber was behind a camouflaged door at the back of the main temple. We walked through the narrow corridor, down, down, down, deep beneath the temple. We reached another door. Inside was a small room made of granite slab. There was a water jug, bowl of rice, toilet bucket, simple bed with a straw mattress and woollen blanket, and a meditation cushion. Master gave me instructions and left me a lighted sandalwood incense stick. He visited every day and lit another incense stick.

I was given a tiny amount of food for the first twenty days. Every time Master visited, he empowered me with his touch. After a while, I felt that my body had become a pure point of awareness, and I only used it when I needed to move. Otherwise, to me, it had disappeared.

After twenty days, I was given no more food but had water. Master continued to empower many different energy points in me. A lot of unusual and intense experiences happened. One was the ability to float out of the dark chamber, above the temple, to many different places.

At fifty days, Master taught me a new practice of gathering the world's evils. It is a dangerous practice that must only be attempted under strict conditions. Everything had to be confronted, absorbed and dismantled. Challenging, indeed. My experience went from bliss to terror. As each challenge was met, my blissful state would return in greater proportions. The process is called, in translation, *Small Death, Big Life*. For the final eight days of this process, my master stayed by my side, but I was unaware of that at the time.

Eighty days had passed, and it was time to slowly return to the physical world. I started drinking small amounts of sweetened rice milk, then fruit, then vegetables. There were more lighted incense sticks to help my eyes adjust to light. Master stayed in the chamber for longer periods and talked about minor matters to connect me with the world again. The day came to leave, and we walked out together."

"That's incredible," said Maliyan. "So, you redid the one-hundred-day fast? Who looked after you this time."

"Master Xiao," said Robert quietly.

"I see," said Maliyan, who knew that Robert's master would not have left his side.

"And one of the other monks brought me what was physically needed," said Robert, "which was not much."

"I have to go now," said Maliyan, "to meet my friend in Sonder. It's marvellous to have you back. Your house has gone from locked and lifeless to brimming with unlocked life again."

Robert bowed and said, "I am in Qi. Qi is in me."*

---

* The story of Robert is based on the real-life Robert Peng. However, some aspects have been altered and added for the Nanima Series.

CHAPTER 41

MISS MARPLE

Deciding to leave Sonder's outside area to the flies, Maliyan went inside. Leteisha and her boyfriend smiled as they held the door open for her and then exited. It was Maliyan's first visit back to Sonder since her move to The Flat, and she people-watched.

I'm like Miss Marple, thought Maliyan humorously.

Miss Marple, from Agatha Christie's detective series, was an older amateur detective (unpaid and often unthanked) who lived in the quaint English village of St. Mary Mead. The village's tearoom was the main gathering place of the rural community, and it was a constant source of useful, inadvertent information for Miss Marple. She was an unlikely detective with her kind, somewhat dithery way, leading her suspects to underestimate her. However, her understanding of human nature was super sharp, and her powers of observation were keen. Her invisibility and preference for blending into the background, combined with her intelligence, solved many a crime. Miss Marple said of herself:

"Really, I have no gifts—no gifts at all—except perhaps a certain knowledge of human nature. Human nature is much the same everywhere, and, of course, one has the opportunity of seeing it at close quarters in a village like this."

— MISS MARPLE (AGATHA CHRISTIE)

CHAPTER 42

WORST FEARS AND BEST DREAMS

"Surely, I will find what I want soon," said Luna. "I keep looking."

"You're not going to find it," said Maliyan.

"That's very pessimistic," said Luna.

Maliyan laughed and said, "You are looking everywhere but in the right place."

Luna rolled his eyes and looked out the window.

"Did you put your back gate in?" asked Luna, changing the subject.

Maliyan treated the council-owned and mowed paddock behind her house as her own backyard. Not only could she look out her windows and watch it spread down to the creek, but she also had many animal visitors because of it. The only problem was that there was no gate. Every time she stood at her fence, her spirit would bound over to the green beyond, but her body got stuck behind the fence. Thus, she asked the owners if she could put a gate in. No skin off their nose.

"You wouldn't believe it," said Maliyan, "but they said no!"

"They must be worried about security," said Luna. "The trouble is when you lock everyone out, you also lock yourself in."

Maliyan smiled in acknowledgement of Luna's wise words.

"Get an above-ground pool ladder and use it as a stile," he suggested.

Encouraged by his own wise words and practical advice, he ventured back to his problem and said, "Where then? Where is the right place to look?"

"Inside," said Maliyan.

She knew she had to be succinct. She probably had two sentences before Luna would switch off.

"I'm not saying you shouldn't leave," said Maliyan, "but wherever you are, unless you journey within, none of it will work."

One sentence down. Still listening.

"You probably think that if you travel inwards, it will confirm your worst fears, and then there will be no hope."

"What fears?" asked Luna cautiously.

"Everything you think you are," said Maliyan. "I can assure you you are not your worst fears. You are more than your best dreams, but you must discover that for yourself."

LIGHTING UP

CHAPTER 43

BIT OF LIGHT

In The Flat:

Last week, Maliyan took the dormant Christmas box from her garage, pulled out the old, single-thread of LED lights, and wound it around the back fence. In the city, it had always looked a meagre light display compared to other houses. However, it unfailingly made its annual trip from dusty box to fence because a simple hello can be as good as throwing a grand party.

Here, in The Flat, Maliyan was surprised that when 9:00 p.m. hit on the first night of the lights being up, they lit up the surrounding paddock and valley with enthusiasm, turning to outright brilliance as the night progressed. The paddock was dark. The creek below was dark. The farm hill opposite was dark. There were no street lights to be seen, and the lights of the neighbouring houses weren't visible from her fence. In all that darkness, the little lights were having a ball.

When it's dark, thought Maliyan, *you don't need a stadium of lights to make a difference. You just need a bit. A bit of light is a powerful thing when all around is lightless.*

The following evening, as Maliyan checked on her blinking lights, she saw that the farmhouse across the valley now had a row of blue lights on its fence. The farmhouse lights and Maliyan's lights seemed to be winking at each other, tentatively flirting. After a while, they got in sync and pulsed their bright togetherness across the valley and into the town, singing:

> Christmas is coming.
> It's a homecoming.
>
> Forget about your worries
> and all of your hurries.
>
> Together, we are bright.
> As one, we are Light.

CHAPTER 44

WATER AND WEED

After scaling her stile (pool ladder) into the back paddock, Maliyan scanned her newly planted garden bed. When she arrived at the rental, there was no difference between the back lawn and the large garden bed. The whole thing was overrun with Kikuyu grass. You couldn't see where the lawn ended and the garden bed started. The only distinguishing feature was a few tough surviving plants with triumphant flowers amongst the long grass in the garden bed.

It's an art as much as a science to weed old, overgrown garden beds. If you poison everything, then you poison everything! Quick, but deadly. However, you will struggle if you try to pull out all the unwanted grass by hand. From decades of neglect, aggressive grass runners become a jungle of undergrowth, grabbing onto everything and becoming an impenetrable mat. Your weeding will simply be a light prune to which the runners will respond with vigorous, renewed growth. What to do?

You have to be patient and selective. Maliyan did a bit of careful poisoning to infiltrate the conglomeration of entwined runners. Some she shovelled out, which is hard physical work. There was lots of watering to soften the soil, so the runners were more responsive to being removed. And there was careful weeding around the surviving plants, which had to be pruned so that she could see what was happening with them. After beginning the planting process, every evening became a ritual of *water and weed*. Water because new plants are not resilient, and weed because old weeds are.

All in all, it's how we should approach people who need help—tact, perseverance, repeat calm handling, and the occasional deadly word or two to eliminate fatal tendencies. You have to work with them. If you blanket-kill everything that is hurting them, they will collapse under the weight of it and run away. Now and again, something needs to be killed quickly. The root cause has to be eliminated. But most of the time, it's the patient weeding out of thoughts that are not beneficial to their well-being. And you must look for the good and wonderful expression already in them and encourage it to grow. It needs room so that it doesn't have to keep fighting all the weeds of thoughts. It takes time, patience, and love.

CHAPTER 45

LIFE KNOWS

As Maliyan ambled through the paddock, she passed the aged care centre and waved at the ninety-four-year-old man pottering amongst his plants. He was the supplier of the plants she put in her garden. He grew various seedlings on his small allotment and gave them to the Country Women's Opportunity Shop next door. They gave the profit straight back to the aged care centre. The Op Shop was in the original rural hospital. The building was about the size of a large house, tiny by hospital standards, but it would have been a lifesaver to many farmers and their families before the freeway made city access viable.

The plants were on the back steps of the Op Shop, and Maliyan scanned them every morning, well before the shop's opening hours, to see if she wanted any additions to her garden. Not only were the plants dirt-cheap, but they were also grown with knowledge and care. Further, they were entirely acclimatised to the area, which is important for plants. It's no good being a northern city garden when you are a southern country one in the ranges. You have to be who you are. Then you won't struggle. In the same way that we should try to eat what is local, we should grow plants that thrive in our locality. When we are in sync with our particular physical environment, it helps us to flourish.

Maliyan returned to the Op Shop later in the day to pay for her "stolen" plants.

"Thank you so much for coming back," one of the friendly country women said.

Maliyan smiled as if to say, *Of course!* She found it amusing that they usually seemed a little surprised she would bother to come back and pay a few dollars for a plant already in her possession.

They might not know I took the plant, thought Maliyan, *but life does.*

No action is unseen.
No word is unheard.
No thought is unnoticed.

No aspiration is unknown.
No kindness is unrecognised.
No progress is unrewarded.

FIREWORKS

CHAPTER 46

FLAT FESTIVAL

December 21st:
It was summer solstice, the maximum tilt of Earth towards the sun. There were still two months of summer's heat ahead, but deep within the Earth and out into its spacious atmosphere, the turning point had been reached.

Although The Flat was in the ranges like Black Forest, it had significantly warmer temperatures than Black Forest because it was not as high above sea level. Once, Luna said it should be hotter if you were higher because you were closer to the sun. Maliyan wasn't sure if he was joking or not.

It was also the evening of The Flat Festival. When a large planned event happens in a country town, everyone goes. In the city, people often feel lonely amongst so many people, but country towns, being more codependent, tend to be more connected. In Yan Yan Gurt (the tiny town twenty minutes out of Nanima where Maliyan's family came from), events in the town hall were terrific fun. Town life was spun around the regular bush dances, balls, New Year's Eve parties, birthdays, twenty-firsts, weddings, christenings, wedding anniversaries, and various other landmark occasions.

The 6:00 p.m. festival parade was about to start. It seemed that half the population was on the sidewalk cheering and waving at their friends, and half were in the actual parade. If you wanted to be in the parade, you could practically step into it, walk along, and start waving to people. There was the scout group, the kinder group, the high school drama group, the high school science group, the aged care residents (dressed up and waving through their van windows), the callisthenics group, the highland dancers, the pipe band (with bagpipes), various charities and community advancement groups, and the Fire Brigade. The groups were interspersed with highlights such as a Chinese dragon, a lady on stilts, antique farm equipment, a monster truck, and a lollie-throwing Santa.

As Maliyan had already been at the festival for quite a while, she decided to walk home before the climatic fireworks. She knew she could see them from her back fence. Once home and sitting outside, she became immersed in the sensation of the falling dusk on the excited town and felt herself being drawn to her dream home.

CHAPTER 47

EARTH-WORKS

Dream Planet:

Maliyan did not go to her residence but to one of the regular meetings that the "parents" or Wise Ones scheduled. This particular meeting was called Earth-Works and was for those who lived on Earth.

"Every night, when you sleep on Earth," said one of the Wise Ones, "you are reconstructing the **reality** you experience in your day-to-day life there. Of course, this concept is incomprehensible to humans who believe their physical existence is innately concrete. Regardless of their beliefs, it is not. It is reconstructed every night so that it will seem a certain way on waking. It is done with their willing cooperation, but most are 100% unaware of this arrangement.

This phenomenon explains why sleep is so high on the list of needs for human survival. First is air, then water, then sleep, then food. This may seem surprising. However, sleep-deprived humans lose their ability to reconstruct a strong physical presence. If they are sleep-deprived for too long, their connection to the material experience of Earth will start dismantling, and they will die of some related physical problem.

Once this idea vaguely crosses the mind of a human, a new dimension will open. If reality is unconsciously constructed every night during sleep, then it can be consciously constructed in a more beneficial and enjoyable way."

AFTER A PAUSE, THE OTHER WISE ONE SPOKE.

"The construction of reality leads to our second point for this meeting, which is the concurrent existence of many **simultaneous realities**. There is not only one reality. There are many, and people (and other types of beings) constantly move between them. Although this is pie-in-the-sky to most humans, they can glimpse it by noting how different their reality looks and feels depending on their mental space. One day, for example, everyone smiles at them and plays into their hands like putty; the next, people insult and abuse them. It is not that it just *seems* different. It is, in fact, a different, concurrent, parallel reality.

Can you see how liberating this is? If you do not like your reality, you can shift to one where things work differently. If you are suffering in one reality, you can move to a better one. It is not even that difficult to do. Firstly, the improved version of reality must be pictured very clearly in your mind. What cannot be conceived cannot be born. Secondly, it must be frequently visited until it no longer seems improbable. It must become familiar and a definite possibility. Gradually, it will move from improbable to possible to likely to inevitable."

. . .

SWAPPING BACK TO THE FIRST WISE ONE, THE EARTH-WORKS
meeting continued.

"Furthermore, as you know, people on Earth see **time** as
linear—past, present, and future. It is not. This can be
understood alongside the previous two topics. When it is
understood that reality is constructed and that there is more
than one reality, the concept of time becomes loose. If one
can move between realities, one can move backwards and
forwards as well.

While we are not encouraging you to explain the concept of
timelessness to humans directly, it helps them to move in
that direction when they examine something that has healed
in their lives. When something truly gets healed, the past
can appear to change. This has happened to many people on
Earth. At some point in their life, they will understand why
someone did something negative (most commonly, it is an
understanding of the other person's suffering), and a
moment of authentic forgiveness will automatically spring
up. Often, after a while, they will look back and can barely
remember what used to irritate and upset them so much.
The "reality" of the past has unbound itself, sometimes
altering the memory, sometimes wholly wiping out the
memory.

What is more, some individuals who used to be a large part
of their life will tend to "disappear" from their experience
(because they don't energetically belong in the new reality),
and others will become more present (because their vibration is more in sync with the new reality).

*A different experience of life
creates not only a different future
but also a different past."*

IN FINISHING THE MEETING, BOTH THE WISE ONES SAID IN perfect unison,

> "On Earth, Christmas is approaching. For many people, it is a time of healing and forgiveness because the individual they call Yeshua or Jesus embodies those qualities in a powerful, energetic form. Although the souls of humans always live in the domain of spirit, they are having a 'dream' that they are on Earth, a dream that they must reinvent each night. Help them to make it a happy dream. It must first become a happy dream before the dream untangles itself and reality dawns in stunning light."

WITH THAT, MALIYAN WAS BROUGHT BACK TO HER GARDEN WITH the bang and fizz of the festival fireworks.

Help them to make it a happy dream, she repeated in her mind as the swish and spark of banging colour lit up The Flat's darkened sky.

STRANGE AND STRANGER

CHAPTER 48
SPIRITUAL STILE

Christmas Day:

TEXT MESSAGE FROM LUNA

Merry Christmas, mi amor.

MALIYAN

You got there safely?

LUNA

Yes, I'm safe.

MALIYAN

Happy Christmas x

LUNA

Sometimes, I wonder why we are friends.

MALIYAN

LUNA

I mean you are not like my other friends.

MALIYAN

What are your other friends like?

LUNA

It's just that I wonder what we have in common.

IF YOU WANT TO FEEL COMFORTABLE, PICK FRIENDS WHO SUPPORT your established identity. That is okay. It is a sensible life arrangement. However, if you want to grow, at least let one person be a challenge. They may not challenge you in words, but their very existence will challenge the structure of your mind. It is uncomfortable, but if it is someone for you, then you won't be able to untangle yourself from them. You will try. It won't work. You will try to fit them into the life you already have. It won't work. It may be unsettling, but you have found someone who is a spiritual stile, an energetic pathway, to your higher self. Don't waste the opportunity. And if you do, don't waste it when it swings your way again.

MALIYAN

Life, Luna. We have LIFE in common.

CHAPTER 49

TRY AGAIN

As he had told Maliyan, Luna was safe. But he wasn't up north. He was still in the southern city near The Flat. He didn't want to tell her yet. The Christmas holidays became a time of introspection. As he lived by himself, he normally had quite a lot of time alone, but he wasn't usually introspective. He was extrospective. He focused on things outside himself. Generally, distractions. If he felt up to socialising, it was other people. Otherwise, it was T.V., books, and watching sports.

He wasn't entirely sure how safe he was in the internal world. It had always seemed murky, confusing, and disconcerting to him. It made him fidgety and compulsive. Nevertheless, something inside him said that it was time, time to journey inward, and that delaying it would only bring suffering, worse suffering. These were strange ideas for Luna, but they didn't feel quite as strange as they used to. The possibility that he could not feel such a stranger in the strange internal world began to emerge.

He had moments of panic, even terror, in his travels, but a voice (someone's voice, he knew not whose) told him that when the fear is at its worst, when it starts throwing bombs at you and conducts a large orchestra with symphonic madness, then it is close to its breaking point. It told him that if he marched through the moments of madness and terror, they would give in and dissolve under the pressure.

When you are closest to making a breakthrough in your personal growth, your fear throws up the greatest intensity. It will do whatever it can to deter you from moving ahead. If you succumb to its frightening and treacherous threats, pick yourself up and try again. If you forget what you are trying to do, try again. If you change your mind and head the other way, try again. With perseverance, your fear will exit the scene, and you will be standing in a new world.

North or south wouldn't make any difference to Luna, but the choice between out and in would be transforming. Instead of the dreaded inner world being the death of him, it could become the death of his relentless, ever-altering fears and the birth of ever-multiplying improvement and peace. A happy death, indeed.

CHAPTER 50

RUNNING WITH THE RIVER

"I've been much better since we talked last," said Bell on the phone.

"You sound much better," said Maliyan.

"What was that place?" asked Bell. "The place you took me to in the meditation."

"Did it seem familiar?" asked Maliyan.

"Yes and no," said Bell.

"Not long after I moved south," said Maliyan, "I drove to the top of Geboor. As I looked down to Black Forest in one direction and the city in the opposite direction, I heard more of the poem that Francis originally read us in the Nanima poustinia. It went like this:

> Look at the town below.
> It is you.
> Look at the city in the distance.
> It is you.
> Every rumbling car and pacing person
> is you.
> Every running child and wagging dog
> is you.
> Look to the far reaches of the ranges.
> It is you.
> Look to the endless sky.
> It is you."

"When you still lived in Nanima," interrupted Bell, "you took some earth from the banks of the Bell, mixed it into a paste with the river's water, put it on your thumb, drew a line down my forehead, and said, 'I name you Bell-Bell. You run with this river.' Do you remember that?"

"Of course," said Maliyan.

"And, in the very same spot, a year-and-a-half later," continued Bell, "on the last day of my retreat with Euroka, he said, 'When you sit with the river long enough—not sleeping, not making things up, just sitting, just being—there is a chance of becoming, a chance of becoming something more until, one day, you become the river.'"

"Yes?" said Maliyan.

"So, am I the river yet?" asked Bell.

Maliyan laughed and said, "You are the town below, the far city, the rumbling car, pacing person, running child, wagging dog, the far reaches of the ranges, the endless sky, and yes, Bell, you are the river. It is you."

As the energy of the Bell River and the thread of Geboor became more a part of Bell, she became less a part of herself (the fabricated, fearful self). Life passionately longs to dissolve that self and is so utterly selfish that it wants absolute possession.

It is you.
It is you.
It is you.

149

The End

THE FLAT

BOOK 4 OF THE NANIMA SERIES

PART I
SIX MONTHS AT A TIME

PAPERBOY

CHAPTER 1

HAPPY DREAMS

"Happy dreams," said Luna as he opened the bedroom door for Iggy to enter.

"Sleep well," said Maliyan as she headed for the bathroom.

"I will," said Luna. "The night is so quiet at your house that I feel like I'm in a cocoon."

He was used to the hustle and bustle, traffic and horns, yelling and late-night laughing of inner-city life.

At the end of his Christmas holiday break, Luna was ready to tell Maliyan that he wasn't in the northern city, but still in the southern one near her. When he initially decided to move back north, he gave notice on his flat. By the time he decided that he was no longer going, his flat had been leased to someone else, so he was homeless. Maliyan offered him her spare room, assuming he wouldn't take it. He did take it. The last time they lived together was summer, two years ago, in Nanima, in the shophouse of Luna Tiks.

CHAPTER 2

STILL ALIVE

In his first week of living in The Flat, Luna visited every cafe in town. He was unimpressed by all, some more than others. The Flat didn't have a happening cafe like Sonder in Black Forest. Its cafes were conventional country ones, at best, clean, pleasant, and running smoothly. None had a vibe—not the vibe that suited Luna.

The worst one was *Paperboy*. It had become old and worn long ago, as had its owner, who was an original paperboy from the area when there was no freeway. The disgruntled man, in his mid-seventies, took a shine to Luna. He was won over when Luna decided to have his coffee at one of the tables and listened to some of his worn-out stories. Luna knew which jokes the man would like—rough and ready, crass and offensive—and that clinched it.

As he left, Luna said, "I've been a cafe owner myself. It's a hard slog."

The paperboy mumbled to himself and then looked hard at his new mate.

"Well, matey, if ever you feel like getting back into it, let me know," said the paperboy. "Before I die, I want to visit Italy. It's been a lifelong dream, but if I don't do it soon, my time will be done."

Luna looked around the cafe with its peeling wallpaper and empty seats. He noticed that the coffee machine was new. The paperboy's eyes, sharper than what he gave away, tracked Luna's gaze and faint interest.

His energy picked up, and he said, "The old one broke. I had to get a new one. Look, buddy, if you are interested, you could have the place for six months for next to nothing and make of it what you can. Then I could go to Italy, and it would still be alive when I return, that is, if *I'm* still alive."

CHAPTER 3

INCLUSIVENESS

After thinking about the paperboy's offer for a few days and discussing it with Maliyan, Luna decided to accept it and became the new, if temporary, owner of Paperboy. He quickly acquired the keys and set about cleaning it. After throwing out a mass of dirty stuff lying around the premises, he stuffed the rest in the back shed. He then bought ten cheap, bright cushions and some potted plants on sale and placed them strategically around the room. He visited the Country Women's Association Op Shop next to Maliyan and found some quaint cups, saucers, plates, and ornaments. By the end of the week, Paperboy was a relatively transformed place.

Now, for the tricky bit—staff. You don't need staff when you don't have customers, but Luna intended to have both. He talked one of his chef friends into coming out to The Flat to cook for six months. Then, he set his mind on winning over the town's young people who would become his rotating hospitality staff. Like moths to a flame, they gravitated to Luna's funny and engaging ways. Even in his mid-forties, he still possessed a coolness that young people are drawn to.

He quickly monopolised the gay community's workbase. A lot

of diverse people came to The Flat, and amongst them was a fairly significant gay population. Being so close to the city, people came who wanted to escape city life but also have access to it. These days, small businesses must be diligent about fulfilling all the increasingly mandated inclusive policies, but Luna was the personification of inclusiveness. Inclusiveness means including someone, as they are, into ourselves. His inclusiveness was what made his relationship with Maliyan possible.

CHAPTER 4

SHAKANA

"I know what the dream planet is called," said Bell on the phone. "I went there in my dream last night, and a Wise One told me. They said it translates as Shakana."

"Really?" said Maliyan.

"The Wise One said that they don't have names for each other or even for their planet because everything is known as energy," said Bell. "However, the word Shakana is close because it means empathic collective consciousness, which is what they are."

In Bell's dream of planet Shakana:

"Breathe in and out three times, slowly," said the Wise One. "As you breathe out, see your mind, consciousness, and soul expanding. Let it grow more each time. Think of yourself as a translucent, giant, blue ball of harmonic, shining energy. Watch as your spread and size increase. You are full of light.

A tiny shape is in the centre of the massive ball of light. It is the shape of a human body. It is your body. It is your body in crystallised form. Contrary to your normal perceptual belief, your mind is not inside your body. It is the other way around. It is your body that is in your mind.

The crystal substance that forms your body can be reformed in a different way. Whenever you expand your consciousness and move your energy beyond your body's boundaries, the material of your physical body can restructure itself more healthily.

Imagine yourself in perfect health. You know what that feels like, don't you? It can be like not feeling anything. Nothing is grating or clunking. Everything is operating smoothly, like an oiled machine. The body becomes silent. Strong and silent. Have a clear image of your body in perfect health, and then, with your consciousness enlarged, imprint that on the crystalline substance that forms your body.

For this exercise to work effectively, repeat it often during your day-to-day Earth life, not because it can't be instantaneous, but because you believe it can't be. The problem is not the process but your ingrained and unconscious belief patterns. Your old belief systems will keep reversing the body back into its preferred, comfortable, dysfunctional version. If you persevere and keep replanting the new ideas, your body will slowly but surely reform and restructure itself, and sometimes, it will make big, sudden leaps."

"THE WISE ONE TOLD ME THAT OUR BODY IS IN OUR MIND, NOT the other way around," said Bell. "How strange to think of it like that."

"Yes," said Maliyan, "and it's not only our body that is in our mind. There is more in our mind than there is *out there*."

CHAPTER 5

QUEERER THAN QUEER

"By the way," said Maliyan as Bell was about to hang up the phone, "Luna is living with me."

"Living with you?" said Bell. "Why?"

"He's working in The Flat for six months."

"Is he staying with you for six months?"

"I'm not sure how long he is staying."

After a pause, Bell said, "I don't think that will work."

"It is working," said Maliyan.

"In what way is it working?"

"In whatever way it decides to work."

"He's gay," said Bell.

"Well then, he won't bother me for sex."

"Is that a good thing?"

"Maybe, maybe not," said Maliyan.

"You might not need it, but he probably does. What if he starts bringing male company home?"

"He won't."

BEFORE LUNA BEGAN STAYING AT MALIYAN'S HOUSE, SHE TOLD him, "I am a highly perceptive and intuitive person, Luna, and I have set up my life so that other people's energy doesn't adversely affect me. My home is my energetic sanctuary. You can be here, but not your friends. Sorry, you need to meet up with them somewhere else."

Although Maliyan understood other people's need to socialise, she had none. That's what happens when you are entirely self-assured on the inside. Your interactions with people become very purposeful and decisive. It's not disengagement. You are totally connected, but it is conscious connection.

"LUNA IS ONLY QUEER IN ONE WAY," MALIYAN SAID TO BELL. "I'M queer in just about every way except that one."

HEALER

FEELER

Whena Maliyan moved to The Flat, she decided to use one of her three bedrooms as a workspace. She hadn't worked for the past three years, since moving to the country. In Nanima, she bought a small home and lived off her savings. She neither needed nor wanted much in the way of material things, so, at a scrape, it was viable, at least, for some years. When she moved to Black Forest, she rented Bell's father's house. Eventually, her Nanima house was sold, and the money was invested. Now that she was in The Flat, she was still renting and had a basic income from her investments. Nevertheless, she decided to go back to work.

Maliyan didn't return to her clerical work of thirty years in the city. She was drawn to something new—healing. It wasn't the money. She wasn't even sure if she would make any money. It was the desire to help, and she found the idea exciting. The field of healing is so obscure that anyone can say they are a healer. The goods speak for themselves. She made an online site and trusted that the right people would find her. They did.

Her healing room had two chairs for clients, a massage table for hands-on healing (or Reiki), a desk, and an area that acted as a sacred space. It had candles, burning oil, incense, chimes, bells, and a few favourite spiritual books and images. In the corner was a rolled-up yoga mat and cushion for yoga asanas, meditations, prayer, and any other spiritual practice that took Maliyan's fancy.

With time, the atmosphere in the room became highly charged from daily spiritual practices, which was exactly what she wanted it to be for prospective clients. Not that Maliyan had guests, but the room would have been too charged for visitors to sleep in. They would have had too many vivid dreams, and many would not have been pleasant. A healing space not only heals but also brings things up to be healed. Luna was somewhat suspicious of the room and never went in it, even when Maliyan sat there. He would stand at the door and talk to her.

Maliyan's clients usually came during the day when Luna was at Paperboy, but occasionally, he was home. Once, Maliyan told him to stay in his room for one hour and be quiet so the client wouldn't know anyone was home. People tend to be very secretive about their problems, although energetically, there is no such thing as privacy.

The next time a client came in the evening, Maliyan said to Luna, "You'll have to go for a walk for an hour."

"I'll stay in my room again," said Luna.

"No, that doesn't work."

"Why? They can't hear me."

"It's energy," said Maliyan. "I need the energy in the whole house to be a certain way."

Insulted, Luna huffed off and banged the door. Not a great start to a healing session.

When the session ended and Luna returned home, Maliyan said, "It's your home too, for as long as you want it to be. I won't book anyone in at night."

Luna nodded and went to his room, and that was that.

CHAPTER 7

BARRY

SWEEP YOU OFF YOUR FEET

Maliyan's first client was Barry, a seventy-year-old deaf man. That was a challenge. How do you communicate concepts to a person who can't hear words?

As it turned out, he was an excellent lipreader from fifty years of practice. He had hearing until he was twenty and then lost nearly all of it with an infection. He was talkative and avoided watching your face if he didn't want to stop talking.

How convenient! thought Maliyan. *If he was in an argument [which he often was with his long-term wife], he could refuse to look at the other person's lips and thus not "hear" them.*

Malayan surmised that he probably only came to her because she offered a large price reduction to pensioners. Nevertheless, it didn't take him long to realise that Maliyan may be useful to him.

"I might be deaf," said Barry, "but I'm not dumb."

"Of course not," said Maliyan.

His life was a mess of drama, blame, anger, and sadness. He had disjointed relationships with all four grown daughters. His wife left him seven years ago. However, he had the demeanour of someone whose spouse had recently abandoned the relationship.

At one point, he mentioned that he was a good ballroom dancer in his late teens.

"Can you hear the beat of music if it's loud?" asked Maliyan.

"Yes, I can hear it a bit with my hearing aid," said Barry.

"What was your favourite music when you danced?" asked Maliyan.

"The Platters!" said Barry.

After quickly searching her music app, Maliyan started playing *Heaven on Earth* by The Platters and turned it to full volume. She jumped up and stretched out her hand to him.

"Come," she said, "let's dance."

There was no problem with him paying attention to her lips now. Surprised and nervous, he nevertheless took her hand and got up. Not sure how much he could hear the beat and how much he could remember the steps, Maliyan assumed she would have to take the lead. However, after a few minutes, Barry's tall, stiff body relaxed and took the lead perfectly in time with the music. They slowly moved around the room for five more minutes.

Then, Maliyan released her hold and told Barry that they would do some healing. He needed to lie down and close his eyes for the healing. As he couldn't see, he also couldn't "hear", so everything had to be transferred energetically, without language cues. When the hands-on healing was finished, Barry wanted to talk more, much more, but Maliyan stopped him.

"See how you go over the next few weeks," said Maliyan, "and we'll talk again if you wish to return."

She didn't need to worry about him wanting to come back. He started messaging her every day. He explained that because he was on a pension, he could only afford to come once a fortnight, and couldn't even really afford that. He asked if he could come and pay later. He asked if he could "drop in" and talk. He went into long explanations about why no one understands him.

I'm sorry for bothering you so much. If you give me a chance, I could sweep you off your feet.

He was entirely inappropriate but harmless. Anyway, Maliyan felt that those who came to her were meant to come. It was not for her to say who would come, what the starting point was, or what steps the person would take for their own healing. Her replies consisted of silence or brief, professional replies.

No, you cannot call in. When you can afford it again, please book a session.

He managed to come a few more times. A senior pension does not allow for "luxuries" such as private professional sessions of anything, even with big discounts. But if people are given things too easily, they will often take advantage of them. The thing will tend to lose its worth, and the recipient will not get what they could have out of it. So, it's a balance.

In his last session, Barry brought a letter he had written to his ex-wife, which had not yet been sent. It was smothered in self-pity. By this stage, Maliyan was able to explain to him that he needed to focus on his wife's needs and feelings if he wanted to restore any sort of relationship with her. Together, they completely reworded the letter.

"Women are good at this sort of thing," said Barry. "Men aren't."

That was the last time Maliyan saw Barry. Maybe things improved with his ex-wife, and he no longer needed help in the same way. Maybe he didn't want to spend his valuable pension on his own growth. Either way, no one ever returns to their previous state of consciousness. It's a process of forwards and backwards. The backwards consolidates growth and allows it to settle into our being. The forwards is for freedom.

CHAPTER 8

CARMEL

LIKE IT LIKE THAT

Another client was a neighbour of Maliyan's who was in her late eighties. She was small in stature and round in diameter, as many older people become. They move less, but their food intake doesn't decrease enough to match their lack of movement. They shrink in height and grow in width. A friendly, grandmotherly sort of woman, Carmel one day asked Maliyan what work she did and then decided to book in.

She walked slowly from next door to her appointment using her walking frame. Although she struggled to walk, she was frequently out and about in her little red car, zooming here and there between her eight children and many grandchildren. She said she couldn't sit still.

"Do you still have your husband with you?" asked Maliyan in the session.

"Not for the last two years," said Carmel.

"I'm sorry to hear that," said Maliyan.

"Don't be," said Carmel. "After sixty-eight years, I left the old fool. I couldn't stand it anymore."

Sixty-eight years is a long time after which to decide that you cannot stand someone anymore, thought Maliyan.

"He's not that bad, I s'pose", said Carmel, "but I wanted my freedom. So, I moved out of our house and rent here."

Carmel was not the sort of person to say mean things about people in general. Maliyan guessed that it was only her husband that she allowed herself to speak about in such a way. She often saw Carmel's children and grandchildren pulling up to or leaving her house. Just yesterday, she heard one of the adult grandchildren yell out their car window, "Love you, Nan!"

"How is it all working then?" asked Maliyan.

"Fine. I still see my hubby a lot. Sometimes, I stay there, and sometimes he stays here. But I can always leave or tell him to leave. And I like it like that."

"Well, why not?" said Maliyan.

"The family home has just been sold," said Carmel. "Half the money is not enough for me to buy around here, so I'll keep renting. But damn fool hubby has bought somewhere way out country, three hours away. Cheaper out there, you see. But who's going to drive three hours to visit him? I guess it'll be me."

"How can I help you today?" asked Maliyan.

Carmel had a long list of physical problems. She wasn't very receptive to new ideas (physical or spiritual), although she had been receptive to the unusual idea of leaving her relatively compatible husband after sixty-eight years. Maliyan did a short healing with Carmel sitting in the chair. She put on soft, conventional music (no chanting, drums, chimes, or ethereal chords) and helped her relax with deep breathing. That was about the best she could hope for at this stage.

Knowing that her body was the most accessible point of helping her, Maliyan said, "Have you ever been to a chiropractor?"

"No," said Carmel. "I'm not into stuff like that. Anyway, I'm going to see the surgeon next week."

"I see," said Maliyan.

Carmel considered the state of her body as an inevitable part of ageing. Maliyan knew it was not. It is possible and highly desirable for people to look after their bodies well enough over a lifetime to avoid many, if not most, illnesses. Old age doesn't have to be frailty, pain, suffering, and a brutal collapse of material existence. It can be gentle, vital, wise, peaceful, and active. The soul can exit the body calmly and efficiently at the right time without undue stress. Carmel was a long way from that, but nevertheless, could be helped with a few simple changes.

"I think you would be surprised how much a chiropractor could help you," said Maliyan. "It wouldn't be an instant fix, but if you went every week, the pain in your body would significantly reduce. I can see how crooked your hips are, and that is causing your sciatica."

Maliyan didn't overload her with more information about how it would help her organs and nervous system, and allow for a better flow of energy along the spine so that her life force would not have to fight itself. Carmel looked unconvinced, but that was her right to be. Healing has to be allowed into one's life, not forced.

CHAPTER 9

CLARA

FROM EARTH AND HEAVEN

Clara was a healer herself. She booked an online session as she could not travel to Maliyan. She cared for her elderly parents in her hometown, which she hated. She hated the town, not her parents, although she increasingly resented having to look after them. Clara was usually very active with many ideas and lots of energy. Six months ago, after accepting an interesting job overseas, she went to say goodbye to her parents. However, she realised she couldn't leave them alone after seeing them. She now felt utterly stuck and resentful (unusual feelings for her).

Maliyan was not sure how receptive Clara was to her help because people in the same profession can sometimes be a little snooty and judgmental of each other. Not that Clara was like that, but her demeanour was slightly guarded. Nevertheless, they talked about the ideas of freedom and honesty and the possible practical ways to resolve the problem. As the session was online, there was no hands-on healing. The healing aspect had to be an entirely nonphysical transfer of energy, negating space and time. At the end of the session, Clara was politely grateful and ended the conversation.

Two weeks later, Maliyan heard from a different Clara altogether. She said it was like a miracle. The entire weight of the situation had lifted, and she felt reconnected to her true self. She got an idea about how to lessen her care duties with her parents and gradually get them used to outside help. Out of the blue, she was offered another wonderful job overseas. It was better than the one she had to decline, allowing her to further her spiritual development. Furthermore, they were willing to wait for her.

Lastly, she said that the strangest thing happened to her bank account. Lack of money was one of her pressing problems due to her inability to work. She didn't even have enough to pay Maliyan the full amount and asked for a discount, to which, of course, Maliyan said yes. From seemingly nowhere, a considerable amount of money landed in her account. She couldn't understand where on earth it had come from. The mysterious money sat in her account for a while, and as no one claimed it, she accepted it as a gift from Heaven. She immediately paid Maliyan the rest of the money, amongst other things.

"I was absolutely overwhelmed when I rang you," said Clara. "I woke up the next day as a new, calm, clear person. The constant anxiety that had been hounding me vanished. I don't know how to thank you."

"That's thanks enough," said Maliyan.

No healer heals anyone. No healer makes miracles. No healer is responsible for anyone's lack of receptivity or unwillingness to change. All a healer can do is get themselves in a healed state, and then it is up to the other person to be inspired to match that vibration or to prefer their misery. It's that simple. That beautiful. That powerful. Miracles are natural when we see life as energy. It is suffering that is so unnatural.

WATERMELON SPECIAL

CHAPTER 10

THE SCONE MAN AND THE PANCAKE LADY

Once a month, The Flat had a town market. Vendors came from near and far. Their diverse range of goods, many handmade with love and natural ingredients, drew a crowd of customers from equally near and far. Maliyan watched as the scone man prepared a large batch of sultana scones for the oven. As she couldn't decide between the scone man and the pancake lady, she bought both, along with some liquorice from the liquorice man and some fudge from the fudge family.

After making her way through the maze of stalls, she weaved through the crowds on the adjoining street. Most of the cafes were busy with the overflow of market customers. She could see Luna through the front window of Paperboy, eyes on the many concurrent tasks of keeping a busy cafe running. People who work in hospitality keep relatively fit from running around all day. They also keep a fit mind as they have to think fast and remember a succession of orders and tasks—fast feet, fast mind—a good discipline.

Although Luna always complained about working in hospitality, it helped him stay on track. He was forced to be positive and engaged, whether he felt like it or not. Left to his own devices, it would have been a great deal more of *not feeling like it*. The survival of his business made him discipline his mind and emotions. In return, hundreds of people felt better for visiting his cafe. He couldn't see that, but one day, he would. Then, he probably wouldn't even have to work in hospitality if he didn't want to. It would have served its purpose. Seeing Maliyan out of the corner of his eye, he sighed. Last night was a restless one.

CHAPTER 11

WATERMELON TOURMALINE

ast night:

It was 4:00 a.m., and Maliyan heard bumping in the kitchen.

"What are you doing?" she asked as she struggled to get her arms into her inside-out dressing gown sleeves.

"I can't sleep," said Luna. "I've been awake for the last hour."

It is no coincidence that many restless sleepers and troubled minds wake between 3:00 and 4:00 a.m. It is a time of high psychic sensitivity. That means that the mind will be working overtime with worries, unresolved issues, and fear. On the other hand, it is also a heightened time of out-of-body travels, lucid dreaming, inspired problem-solving, and brilliant ideas. Some of our most innovative scientific discoveries have come from 3:00 a.m. dreams and visions.

If you are the former, not the latter (the restless, not the inspired), you most likely won't want to wake up. You will be trying to get back to sleep, which won't work.

"Is anything bothering you?" asked Maliyan coaxingly.

"Nothing," said Luna. "Nothing at all."

"Okay. Well, what have you been thinking about for the last hour? You must have been thinking about something."

"If you must know—watermelon juice special."

"Hmm?"

"We have a watermelon juice special at Paperboy, and I can't get it out of my head."

Maliyan put the kettle on for herbal tea and said quietly, "You know, love, when a thought won't stop circling in our head, it really has nothing to do with the thing that is circling."

Luna looked doubtful but also desperate.

"How do I get rid of it?" he asked.

"Don't try to get rid of it. Listen to it."

Luna's attention was fading. Maliyan touched his arm, and he raised his head.

"I just want it to stop," he said. "I have to work tomorrow."

"I understand," said Maliyan, "but the watermelon is covering for something."

"Covering something? What sort of something?"

She could easily have told him what was "wrong" and what it was covering, but what good would that have been? Evolution has to happen by personal experience, not by someone telling us. Otherwise, it is powerless.

"I'm not sure," said Maliyan. "But you will know. Let it come up when it is ready. The watermelon is trying to help you."

"I'll try," said Luna with a sigh as he walked back to his room, herbal tea in hand. "I guess it will show its true colours when it's ready."

◈

The next morning, Maliyan passed Luna a small crystal before he went to work.

"What is it?" asked Luna.

"Watermelon tourmaline," answered Maliyan.

Luna held it to the light and said, "It's pink in the middle and green on the outside, like watermelon."

"Yes, the two colours of the heart—pink and green," said Maliyan. "It connects with the emotional centre."

After picking up the box that the crystal came in, Luna read:

Watermelon tourmaline will help you connect with your feelings. It will soften the emotional space around you and bring closeness to your relationships.

He put it in his pocket and kissed her goodbye.

CHAPTER 12

POPPING THE SEED

Although he momentarily considered it, Luna didn't deep dive into an emotional-heart transition. Instead, he left the watermelon tourmaline on the kitchen bench and got mean. That's one of the things that can happen when someone's higher self tries to talk to them but gets ignored.

It's like squeezing a watermelon seed. How much pressure does a watermelon seed need to pop? How much pressure can a person tolerate before releasing themselves to change? Obviously, Luna was not ready to pop. He ignored Maliyan's suggestion. He tried to ignore his watermelon juice special obsession. He tried to ignore everything. But nothing ignored him. He started feeling worse and worse about himself. And when he got mean to himself, he could also get mean to others.

One of his favourite negative things in that state was to talk about his many other friends. With each additional reference to the long list of "important" friends, Maliyan got further and further down the list. If she had let him, he would have got so dismissive that she would have ended up as a worm (no offence to worms). But she didn't let him. It is one thing to understand that someone's destructive behaviour stems from their loathing of themselves. It is another to accept that behaviour towards oneself. And so, Luna and Maliyan lived in the same house but in disconnected worlds.

CHAPTER 13

DORIE'S CAFE

A week later:

It was nearly 7:00 a.m. as Maliyan passed Paperboy on her morning walk and headed further down the main street to *Dorie's Cafe.*

WHEN SHE MOVED TO THE FLAT, IT TOOK MALIYAN QUITE A while to visit Dorie's Cafe because it looked so ordinary. It was clean and ordered but outdated, personality-less, and empty. Although it had many rows of indoor and outdoor tables ready for customers, less than 10% of those intended customers ever showed up.

One day, when everything else was closed, Maliyan went into Dorie's Cafe. Dorie was plain in appearance and thought, but humble and kind, and had a natural country feel for what was healthy. The food in the shop was made on the premises by Dorie's husband, so it was fresh and essentially homemade. Dorie told Maliyan that she preferred organic fruit for her shop juices, but it was too expensive. Sometimes, she brought in fruit and vegetables from her own large garden.

"Not enough rain for them to grow well this year," said Dorie.

She chatted with her longtime customers about their families, work problems, and health issues. She was a cheerful, nonjudgmental listener and tried to add little, inane jokes here and there to bounce the conversation along. At one point, the cafe, which opened forty years ago, would have had all the tables and chairs fully occupied.

❧

ON HER SECOND VISIT TO DORIE'S CAFE, MALIYAN WAS ASKED IF she would like a coffee card.

"Sure," said Maliyan.

The hundred or so coffee cards were marked with the customers' first names and kept in a small box on the counter. Once in the box, you were not forgotten.

When Maliyan tried to use the restroom, the automatic motion-detector lights wouldn't detect her. Dorie came to the rescue, and the light turned on immediately.

"You must be a nobody," Dorie said with a chuckle.

She covered her mouth and apologised as if that was a rude thing to say. Rude wasn't in Dorie's makeup. Anyway, there was some truth in Dorie's comment. The detectors could not pick up the form of Maliyan's body. Sometimes, the same thing happened with automatic doors in shopping centres. They couldn't "see" Maliyan, and she would have to wait for someone else to approach the door. Further, Maliyan's fingerprint identity was frequently not recognised on her laptop.

When people are in the process of changing their energetic structure, the normal, physical, Earth-world cues can be missing, reconfigured, or jumbled. You can become a "no-body" in one domain and a somebody in another. The physical body can melt, while the etheric one grows.

❧

Back to this morning:

6:00 to 7:00 was tradie time at all the cafes—tradies and early walkers. The front window of Dorie's Cafe faced the sunrise. The pink cloud wisps peeked through the forest-green, causing a watermelon glow. Golden orbs of sunlight stretched their fingers into Dorie's space.

"Bit bright this morning," said Dorie with mild complaint.

"Bloody boss," said an overweight, ageing tradie, interrupting the peace.

He shook his head in disgust as he leaned on the counter and waited for his coffee. Dorie nodded in commiseration.

"Been at it again," said the man. "Always jumping from one thing to another. Never there when we need him. This week, you wouldn't believe it. He started a breathing class here in The Flat. Bloody breathing. I think I know how to breathe, thank you very much!"

The man's belly bobbed around as he laughed in condescending annoyance.

"Tsk, tsk," said Dorie quietly.

She probably also had no idea why someone would need to learn breathing.

"Did you do well with the market crowds last week?" asked Maliyan after the tradie left.

"No, these days we don't open on the weekends," said Dorie with a shrug. "Can't get any staff."

Luna has no problem getting staff for the weekend, thought Maliyan, but that was the last thing she would tell her. *Dorie has had her day of business success. Now, she makes a living in a minimally stressful way, and isn't that success enough? Isn't being rich being able to live how we truly want? Life can give us what we need in many more ways than just money.*

CHAPTER 14

MAIN STREET MEN

Following the 6:00 to 7:00 a.m. tradie time was the 7:00 to 8:00 *Main Street Men* time. That's what Maliyan called them, anyway. Next door to Dorie's Cafe was another cafe that always had a rowdy group of men aged 50 to 70 who commandeered the outside tables and, to an extent, the whole street. They looked and sounded like builders, plumbers, rescue workers, and other manly jobs, the sort of men who would volunteer for the local C.F.A. (Country Fire Authority), who ran towards fires when everyone else ran away from them. They must have been shift workers, retired, or currently unemployed to afford the luxury of sitting with their mates for an hour every morning.

They told each other stories, jokes, and the occasional bit of news from home. Sometimes, they got carried away with themselves, and you could hear, up and down the street, raucous laughter and snippets of "...chased the f***ing bird...slammed the f***ing door...f***ing fell over...etc." No doubt it was good for their mental health. Men that age can do with a good laugh.

If met on their own along the walking tracks, every one of those men would have politely smiled at Maliyan and said, "Good morning." But here, in the aging schoolyard, they seemed somewhat socially clumsy. They would have responded if Maliyan had stopped and spoken to the group. However, they would have responded with the pack mentality of males viewing females as entertainment. No, thanks. So, every morning, she kept walking.

CHAPTER 15

ORCHESTRA

After passing the Main Street Men, Maliyan headed for the most forested section of the walking track next to the creek. It was the first week of autumn, and there was a hint of leaves turning colour. The gravel track made a crunching noise as she went deeper into the grove of oak, cypress, and pine trees—crunch, crunch, crunch. The leaves glimmered as they caught the morning light. Some had a silver backing and turned backwards and forwards like majestic tinsel. Next to the track, the creek jumped here and there over the rocks and through the weeds. It took the path of least resistance around and through the obstacles—bubble, bubble, bubble.

One of the oak trees seemed to be calling. Acorns, mostly green, lay on the ground around it. The magnificent tree emanated a mesmerising, powerful quality. It was partly covered with ivy, making it even more picturesque. Maliyan sat beside the tree, faced the creek, and leaned her back on the trunk. It felt solid and immovable, as if nothing could faze it—as solid as a rock, as solid as the Earth.

Sitting cross-legged against the oak, looking at the lively creek, Maliyan listened. At first, she couldn't hear much. Then, she noticed the wind playing with the leaves of the oak. The wind picked up its intensity, and the leaves moved more energetically—swish, swish, swish. The movement of the leaves harmonised with the bouncing creek—bubble, bubble, bubble.

A new instrument entered the symphony. It was Maliyan's heartbeat. Ba-boom, ba-boom, ba-boom. Leaves, creek, heart. Swish, swish, bubble, bubble, ba-boom, ba-boom. Then, Maliyan's breath joined the orchestra. Breathing in, breathing out. YH (inhale), WH (exhale). Gently and calmly. YH-WH. YH-WH. All four aspects of nature—tree, water, heartbeat, breath—swish, bubble, ba-boom, YH-WH.

As Maliyan breathed out carbon dioxide, the tree breathed it in. As the tree breathed out oxygen, Malayan breathed it in. She breathed out, the tree breathed in, and her spirit seemed to travel into the tree along with the carbon dioxide—into the leaves, along the branches, down the trunk, and into the roots. The oak tree roots were connected to all the other tree roots along the creek. There was an entire root city underground, busily going about its business of transferring food and water and communicating with each member. All was one grand and complex orchestra.

❧

On the way home, Maliyan noticed that Luna had taken down the watermelon juice special sign.

Later that day, he bounced in happily, an hour and a half later than usual, and said, "I went for a swim after work and lay in the spa for ages. The water did wonders for me."

With that, he picked up the watermelon tourmaline and took it to the sanctuary of his room.

SPLITTING PRISM

BE GONE

Two months of autumn had passed in the cool temperate climate of the ranges. The deciduous trees had had their climactic show of red, orange, and yellow. The winds were now scattering the leaves with be-gone dismissiveness to the far corners of the district.

After speaking with Maliyan at the beginning of the year about Luna's presence in her house, Bell went downhill. Her few connections were long, passive-aggressive messages of psychological explanations, threats to withdraw to "protect" herself, condescending advice about ways in which Maliyan could be more helpful to people, information about how to approach neurodivergent people, and the proper way to affirm and love people in general. They were the masked words of attack.

Bell was such a reactive time-bomb that all Maliyan could do was send a heart emoji, which could have meant anything, thus disarming the escalation. A lesser-aware person would have caved through intimidation, lack of psychological/neurodivergent knowledge, or low self-esteem. A more combative person would have instantly fired up in response to Bell's arrogant and antagonistic approach, and an outright battle of insults would have ensued.

Maliyan wondered how such an intelligent person could possibly imagine that her approach (particularly to Maliyan, who clearly cared for her) was a good idea.

Most of Bell's relationships were based on the other person caving, hostile battles, psychological back-patting, uneasy truce, or avoidance. For all Bell's talk of love, she had minimal awareness of Maliyan. She put it down to Maliyan being "closed and unsharing", and said as much. However, a self-assured person does not share in the hope of scraps of love. Sharing is earned by the other's care, which is communicated almost entirely nonverbally. Bell's current approach was doing her far more harm than facing the fear and sense of unworthiness underneath it.

CHAPTER 17

SHUNYATA

On planet Shakana, in Maliyan's dream:

"Hello, Maliyan," said the Wise One telepathically.

"Hello," said Maliyan. "Do you have a name I can call you?"

"Call me Shunyata," said the Wise One. "It means *nothingness*, not in the sense of being absent, but in the sense of fluidity. Nothing sticks to me. I am the feminine half of the Wise Ones."

"Hello, Shunyata," said Maliyan, pleased to have a name.

"Do you remember when we told you about different concurrent realities, last year by your time measurement?" asked Shunyata.

"Yes," said Maliyan. "There is not just one reality, but many simultaneous ones. Although I must admit, that's a difficult concept to get one's head around."

"We understand that," said the Wise One, "but the more you play with the idea, the more sense it will make."

"I have already had glimpses of that," said Maliyan.

"In the version of Earth you are currently experiencing," said Shunyata, "there will be a major splitting of realities."

"What do you mean?"

"Many humans who have chosen Earth, at this time, have done so because they wish to assist in the shift," said Shunyata.

Maliyan's mind went blank. As that tended to happen in the presence of the Wise Ones, she wondered if they purposely blanked out the person's mind so that they were more receptive to new and challenging information.

"Earth is in the process of evolving in two distinct directions," continued Shunyata. "To be accurate, it is evolving in many directions, but for the sake of simplicity, there are two main ones. One is in the positive direction of our planet, ultimately leading to a physical connection between Shakana and Earth and many other advanced planets. The other direction is problematic and may lead to the destruction of your Earth."

"The destruction of which Earth?" asked Maliyan.

"The Earth which is inhabited by those experiencing that particular reality. As I said, there are many versions in between, but these two are the opposing goal posts."

"That sounds... important," said Maliyan.

"Currently, most people on Earth can see both worlds," said Shunyata, "but there is a divider field that could be likened to a glass wall between them. Most people can still choose which side they prefer. With time (as you perceive it), the wall will thicken and become less penetrable."

"Then what?"

"The chasm between the two Earths will broaden, and each version will accelerate towards its future."

"Does that mean we won't see the other goal post anymore?"

"Correct."

"Does it also mean that some people will disappear for us?"

"Yes, it does. Even at this stage, I am sure you have experienced people disappearing from your life out of vibrational incompatibility."

Maliyan thought about people who had disappeared out of her life in that way and wondered what version of Earth they were living on.

"Eventually, in the far distance," said Shunyata, "one version of Earth will become as evolved as we are, where everyone lives peacefully, lovingly, and with a constant experience of happiness, connection, and excitement for life."

"I'm definitely buying that ticket," said Maliyan.

"We hope so," said Shunyata.

Maliyan's smile faded as she thought of her current vibrational incompatibility with Bell.

"Do not grieve the splitting prism," said Shunyata. "People have the freedom to choose the vibration of Earth they want. They are loved by life and can go wherever they wish, positively or negatively. People often have to deeply experience the effect of their choices before kicking goals in the other direction. Be reassured that if your vibration is incompatible with someone else's and they do not want your help, then a splitting of some sort is the best solution. They must choose the world they want to live in. They may not realise that the world they see is their choice, but that does not change that it is."

"Who *will* choose my side of the glass?" asked Maliyan.

"Ahh, we don't want to spoil *all* your surprises," said Shunyata.

CHAPTER 18

NO TRY, NO GOAL

Feeling that she was moving away from Shakana and returning to Earth, Maliyan held onto the edge of Shunyata's flowing gown.

"One last thing," said Maliyan. "Can you come to me during the day, not just in my dreams. That would be great."

"No," said Shunyata. "You are not ready. You might think you are, but you are not. Our vibration is so much higher than yours, so much more intense, that if we approached you during your waking consciousness, you would go into psychic shock."

"What is that?"

"When an evolved being approaches a lesser-evolved one, the lesser one can experience the contact as energetically overwhelming. All the unresolved issues and blockages in the person will instantly surface as if a magnet is pulling them out. The abrupt force of the experience will be unmanageable, and the person will go into fight or flight mode. They will perceive it as dying. They are not dying, although something does die. The person will usually experience the process with terror. You are in your higher energy state when we come to you in your dreams and meditations. We lower our vibration significantly, and then a meeting in the middle is possible."

"I guess that type of fight or flight reaction can happen between humans, too," said Maliyan.

"Yes," said Shunyata, "if you try to help someone who is not ready, they will run away or fight for survival. That is why respecting people's decisions is vital. Otherwise, you can send them into a version of psychic shock."

"But if I don't try..." said Maliyan

"Intuition and wisdom will guide you," said Shunyata. "And we are closer than you imagine."

THROWING SHADE

CHAPTER 19

RIPE AND READY

I*n Paperboy:*

"Ooooh," Luna said to Maliyan, casting his eyes in the direction of a good-looking male customer, who was exiting with his takeaway. "He's ripe for the picking."

As was her general response to such comments, Maliyan ignored him.

Unsatisfied with her non-engagement, Luna persisted, "Don't you think?"

"I don't know," said Maliyan. "Is he? I guess."

Most days, Maliyan called into Paperboy. By now, Luna had formed a close and lively friendship circle with staff members. Taking his cue, they were consistently positive towards her. There were a few gay male customers who were suspicious of her intentions and somewhat jealous of her living arrangement with Luna. They could throw a bit of shade.

Over the past week, every time Maliyan went into Paperboy, Luna made a show of pointing out attractive men to her. Yesterday, he said, "Dayum, somebody call the fire department," when a local firey came in. The day before, he said, "I don't chase men, but I'd

207

trip and fall on that one." Another day, "He's hotter than my ex's karma." Each time he made the comments, he said them to Maliyan within earshot of one of the shady gay men.

CHAPTER 20

ENBY

That evening, at home:

"Some of my friends have been commenting about you lately," volunteered Luna.

"Gay friends?" asked Maliyan.

"Uh-huh," said Luna.

"What sort of comments?"

"'Not your usual playlist, hmmm?'" said Luna.

Maliyan laughed and said, "What did you say back?"

"Jealousy's not your colour, babe."

"Did that help?"

"Only for a second."

Maliyan thought for a moment and said, "Tell them I'm non-binary."

"Nah, that won't make any difference," said Luna. "I say you're my housemate."

A FEW DAYS LATER, AT PAPERBOY:

"Enjoy your oat chai," said Phoenix, as they placed it on the table.

"Oooh, I like your new haircut," said Maliyan.

Phoenix now had a bleach-blonde buzz cut. It perfectly suited their casual look of loose shirt, fitted pants, no makeup, and clean, symmetrical face.

"Thanks," said Phoenix.

"I didn't ever think a buzz cut would work on me, but I always wanted one," said Maliyan.

"Are you enby,*too?" asked Phoenix, glancing in Luna's direction.

Maliyan wasn't sure if they were indicating where they got that information or checking to see if Luna needed them.

"Maybe it's monk DNA from a past life," said Maliyan. Not wanting Phoenix to feel abandoned, she added, "Or maybe I prefer to mix things up so that no one takes anything for granted."

---

* Enby means non-binary.

CHAPTER 21

TWO-SPIRIT

Satisfied with the idea that people shouldn't take things for granted, Phoenix took the empty cup away, and Maliyan recalled a conversation with Shunyata.

"The current identity diversity on your planet," said Shunyata, "is helping to break apart destructive, limiting beliefs, which will hold Earth back if not dismantled."

"I guess everyone who is 'different' must have agreed to help with that process," said Maliyan.

"Absolutely," said Shunyata. "Although your current diversity may be somewhat bewildering and even frightening to some humans, it is making way for even greater diversity."

"Such as?" asked Maliyan.

"One day, when you have evolved enough and can cope, humans will come to know that there are many other beings of limitless variety out here in the great unexplored frontier."

"I guess it's not really unexplored," said Maliyan. "It's only unexplored by us."

"Yes, and believe me, when humans start to see the bewildering diversity out here, their small human differences will seem like child's play."

❧

WHEN PAYING, MALIYAN TOLD PHOENIX, "I'VE HEARD THAT some indigenous people in North America say that someone who has both masculine and feminine qualities is a Two-Spirit."

"Two-Spirits are healers," said Phoenix.

"They're older than the oldest stories," said Maliyan.

"Ancient as the ancestors," said Phoenix.

"Old-school sacred," piped up Luna, who had excellent hearing.

"Forever fierce," grinned Phoenix to Luna.

"Original edition," shot back Luna. "Limited release."

DOING IS THE DIALECT

CHAPTER 22

SOMEONE SHOULD

Maliyan closed her front door, dumped her dance clothes on the floor, cut up some vegetables for an early dinner, and made a cup of tea. She was hungry and tired. As she slid the vegetables into the oven to roast, she heard a large thumping sound and falling objects. It was coming from the top driveway she shared with her neighbour, Carmel, who once came to her as a client.

Looking through the window, she saw a dump truck unloading about 3 m² of firewood. It sprawled across the entrance of both houses. Next to the woodpile was Carmel's "estranged" husband, Robert, who, like Carmel, was in his late 80s. Carmel recently had an operation, and he was staying with her during the recovery. Maliyan had talked to him several times, and he was a delightful, kind, and caring man with a lot of natural wisdom. Even though Carmel's decision to separate after sixty-eight years of marriage would have been tough for him, he accepted it, held nothing against her, and got on with life.

Lucky I'm already home from my class, thought Maliyan, *or I wouldn't be getting into my driveway.*

She put on some track pants, took a sip of tea, and again looked out the window. Robert had started carrying the wood into Carmel's garage. Maliyan glanced at her clock—one hour until dusk. She watched Robert's functioning and determined but clearly ageing body, and sighed her hungry tiredness into her by-now warm lounge room air. She looked out the window for a third time at her neighbours' houses, which contained several strong men.

Are they going to let him struggle with the wood on his own, at his age, at this time of the day? Someone should help him, she thought.

Sometimes, Shunyata said,

"Action is the native tongue of Earth."

Maliyan assumed she meant that on other planets and dimensions where physicality was either absent or quasi-present, helping could take many nonphysical forms. But on Earth, because we are a physical planet, our helpfulness needs to be grounded in actually *doing something.* Doing is the dialect of our world.

CHAPTER 23

CRACKING THE CODE

"I've come to help," said Maliyan, showing Robert her garden-gloved hands.

He smiled and didn't say no. One of their neighbours, a man in his thirties, got into his expensive car and backed out of his driveway. Maliyan waved, but he purposely didn't look in their direction.

"I thought we were only getting 1 m²," said Robert, surveying the massive wood pile. "Thanks for helping. It's good to have friends. We'll both throw it into the wheelbarrow, I'll wheel it into the garage, and then we'll make a wood stack. Two hands make light work."

Maliyan wasn't sure it would make light work of this pile, but what else could they do but start and then keep going?

Once in the rhythm of moving wood, Robert started chatting. Even after living in Australia for nearly seventy years, he still had an Irish accent. He came as a twenty-year-old man with his thirty-year-old brother and family.

"Back then, when you were twenty, you were a proper man," said Robert. "There was no mucking around. You had to support yourself and, before long, a young family."

Although Maliyan suggested they not pile too much wood into the wheelbarrow because it would be too heavy, he insisted, "I'll be right."

"I had such poor schooling," explained Robert, "that when I left school at thirteen, I couldn't read or write. For some reason, I couldn't pick it up, and back then, if you didn't catch on, you were put at the back of the class and forgotten about."

Even now, his words had a sting in them.

"When I came to Australia," he said, "I tried to teach myself to read and write, but it was a struggle. I was trying to learn one word at a time. Once my kids were at school, I watched how they were being taught phonics, which is connecting letters with sounds and blending them together to make a word. So instead of memorising whole words, I learned the secret of sounding them out. I cracked the code of language!"

CHAPTER 24

VYING VORTEXES

"My brother and I ended up working as jail wardens," said Robert. "We both spent the rest of our working lives in one or other prison."

The quickest route to the coast from The Flat passed a maximum-security prison. Whenever Maliyan drove by it, she felt an uncomfortable twenty-kilometre radius around the prison, which vibrated with negative energy. It was not just the prison's current energy but the accumulated energy from its history. It was a negative vortex of fear, anger, despair, isolation, and meaninglessness.

The countryside around the prison was notably ugly—flat, cactus-ridden, treeless, dry, and depressing. The open environment was no doubt useful in providing clear sight lines for security and surveillance purposes, but it significantly increased the downward pulling effect of the vortex.

The great saving grace was that to the northwest of the prison, and within its line of sight, was a series of granite ridges, the You Yangs, starkly contrasting the otherwise flat terrain. The You Yangs were a sacred spine of stone and created a powerful positive vortex counteracting the negative vortex of the prison.

There are innumerable energy vortices around the world. Some hold tremendous power, such as Uluru (the sandstone monolith rising majestically from the flat desert plain of Central Australia), but most are comparatively small. Nevertheless, small vortices can still greatly impact our health and sense of well-being. Although we may not know where all the vortices are, we can intuitively find them by living where we feel happy and aligned. Vortices are free energy devices that generate enormous energy without fuel or input, so it's wise to use them.

Some locations can negatively impact us. For example, the high-amplitude, low-frequency vortex of Las Vegas is disturbing to peace seekers. However, it is possible that, by contrast, a person may wake up to their inner light by being saturated with the artificial, outward-pulling, illusory light of the mirage-like city.

CHAPTER 25

BURNT BLESSING

"When we started at the jails," said Robert, "the death penalty was still operating."

The overloaded wheelbarrow swayed from side to side, but he managed to correct it.

"I saw a lot of dead bodies," he said quietly. "Sometimes, I was on duty in the death yard, the exercise yard for condemned men."

"Oh dear," said Maliyan. "Did you talk to them?"

"Back then, you weren't allowed to talk to the prisoners. You'd get in big trouble if you did. But, to me, they were all just men, not bad men, just people. And I never had any problems with them. Sometimes, I'd say something when I was in the death yard, but we weren't there to comfort them. We were there to make sure they didn't commit suicide before the state hanged them."

That thought was enough to silence them both for several minutes.

"Will we take a break?" suggested Maliyan, gazing at the bottomless pile.

"No, love. You go on inside, but I'll keep going because it'll still be here when I come back out."

As Maliyan continued carting wood, Robert continued talking.

"Some of the men should never have been in prison. Some were in the wrong place at the wrong time. Worse people were walking around free than some who ended up in jail."

"Did anything funny ever happen?" asked Maliyan.

Robert shook his head. "No, nothing funny ever happened."

Maliyan felt that some funny things must surely have happened to both prisoners and wardens, but right now, they had escaped Robert's memory.

Carmel slowly struggled out with her walker and apologised for not helping.

"So lazy!" said Maliyan.

Carmel either wasn't in the mood for a joke or didn't appreciate Maliyan's sense of humour and went back inside with Robert's assurance of, "We're fine, darlin'. Go back inside where it's warm."

"For my first ten years in the prisons," said Robert," I tried to be what I thought wardens were supposed to be. One day, when I came home, Carmel said, 'I don't know where the man I married has gone.' After that, I decided to be myself at work. If they didn't like it, they could sack me. Being someone else was making me miserable."

Another neighbour, a man in his forties, walked past with his two small dogs. He waved hello and pointed to the dogs and the fast-fading light to indicate he couldn't stop to help.

"For a long time, my older brother was a mail censor," said Robert. "He would approve or reject incoming and outgoing prisoner mail. Letters were rejected if suspicious, dangerous, or against prison rules. Sometimes, he would take letters back to the men and say, 'Look here, son. You can't say that to your wife. Fix it up, and then I'll approve it.' Although the prison didn't care about saving marriages, my brother probably saved many!"

As the colours in the western sky dimmed and the blackness encroached, Robert and Maliyan swept away the last of the wood scraps from the driveway. Maliyan then returned to her cup of tea (which was dead cold) and her forgotten vegetables in the oven. They were as black as the night sky outside. She took the smoking tray out of the oven, rescued a few edible potatoes, made a new cup of tea, put some toast on, sat down, and felt that everything was perfectly fine, regardless of burnt dinners.

PART II
TIME IS UP

FORMULA

CHAPTER 26

DO SOMETHING

One early July evening:

Six months had passed since Luna began living with Maliyan and the paperboy had "loaned" him the cafe.

"Have you heard anything from the owner of Paperboy?" asked Maliyan.

"Nothing," said Luna.

"Has he returned from Italy yet?"

"No idea."

"Hmm, what's the plan then?"

Luna shrugged and started making dinner.

After he had eaten, Maliyan tried the conversation again.

"What is it you would like to do?" she asked.

"I would like to do something different, but I have to support myself."

"What sort of something?"

"For one thing, I'd like to own a bit of land so that I could be outside."

"You have to be proactive about what you want," said Maliyan. "Otherwise, nothing will happen."

The winter night air was setting in. She turned the heater up and added, "It's fear."

"I'm afraid of having no money!" said Luna.

"You have greater fears," said Maliyan. "Like being laughed at."

"Don't you ever care what people think about you?"

"No. It's my life, not theirs. Besides, most people are in no position to be the judge of anything."

CHAPTER 27

IN SYNC WITH SYNCHRONICITY

"Even if I did decide to follow my dreams," said Luna, "my dreams are not going to fund themselves."

"There's another part to the 'follow our dreams' formula," said Maliyan. "We have to follow them in a way that serves other people. Then, one way or another, our dreams will serve us."

"The only serving I know is hospitality."

"That is a belief, not a truth. You don't know what you are capable of until you try. You could organise the cafe schedule so that you had more time to investigate other things. That way, you could test the water and gradually learn to swim in some new medium."

"If I don't work enough at the cafe, I won't have enough money to test any water. I'll be dead. I'll drown."

Maliyan laughed and said, "That is another belief, that abundance means money. Money is only one way for life to give you what you need. There are many other ways. Imagination is one. Time is another. People giving you something is a third. (Didn't the old paperboy give you his cafe for virtually nothing?) And exchange is another one."

Becoming a little excited by the notion that there could be some validity in the idea, Luna offered, "Relationships are built on exchange—money, sex, children, a home, company, love, whatever turns people on."

"Exactly," said Maliyan. "And probably the most important way that life gives us what we need is synchronicity."

"You're losing me on that one," said Luna.

"When we follow our passions, and use them to serve other people, and don't insist on how everything should turn out, life organises the right timing, the right people, the right place, and the right result."

When Maliyan was going to bed, she said, "One more thing, Luna."

"Yes?"

"I have been thinking that when it is spring, I would like to buy a house again. It won't be much because I want to keep some money invested."

"Oh," said Luna, surprised. "I hadn't thought about *you* moving. I guess I've been thinking about what *I* will do. That's selfish, isn't it?"

"You are trying to sort yourself out," said Malayan tolerantly.

Tolerance, however, does not change the need for each person to fulfil their destiny. Maliyan had her own destiny to meet and had to trust that whatever came to her or went from her would work in a positive way, even if it didn't appear so at the time.

"I'll look for somewhere in The Flat," said Maliyan.

Life moves, and we need to move, too. If we understand the synchronistic nature of existence, we'll move in sync with it. If not...then, we'll learn.

YAN YAN GURT

CHAPTER 28

SAFETY RATE

Maliyan's Uncle Clarence, on the family farm in Yan Yan Gurt (twenty minutes out of Nanima), had been ill and was now recovering. Getting close to ninety, his recovery was probably only going to be partial. So, Maliyan decided to visit him.

Rather than take the small plane to Thubbo, she had the idea to take a slow drive up the beautiful coastal road to the northern city (thirteen hours drive time). Then, she would cross the mountains to drive out west to Nanima (an additional five-hour drive). From Nanima, she would travel to see her uncle a few times before using the faster inland freeway back south again to The Flat (nine hours drive time).

Normally, her trips were well organised in advance, but she wanted this one to be entirely open to synchronicity. She planned neither how long she would be away, how much she would drive each day, where she would stay each night, nor anything else in between. She let synchronicity do all the planning.

When she felt tired from driving, she stopped—sometimes in country towns, sometimes next to a river, park, or forest. Not all the stops were idyllic, although most were. One stop, brought on by a sudden pang of hunger, was in a town which Maliyan assumed would be lovely because it served as a gateway to the natural beauty of a large lakes area and an alpine region.

When Maliyan parked her car, she headed for the grand old building she had just driven past, thinking it would lead to other pleasant buildings. It was a distinctive bluestone Federation structure, with towers reminiscent of European castles and intricate carvings of Australian flora and fauna around its perimeter. However, as she circled the building, Maliyan felt that she was being circled by a group of drug-addled, dishevelled, glassy-eyed folk who seemed to have nothing better to do. It was a courthouse, and today was hearing day.

She wove her way through the crowd, waited at the nearby traffic light, and listened to a sixty-year-old man who was trying to talk his lawyer into getting him out of some predicament. The lawyer was not much more than a boy. He barely looked old enough to have finished law school, and his bored, vacant face indicated little hope for the man's enthusiastic, if muddled, pleas for assistance.

Searching for food was equally undelightful. Every shop looked dirty, and the food options consisted of highly processed, fatty, and old-looking selections that would be more beneficial not to eat than eat. On that note, Maliyan let synchronicity lead her out of the town. She later discovered it had one of the highest crime rates and lowest safety rates in the state. Hungry but unaffected, she recalled Shunyata's glass wall, which, although invisible, had a spotless safety record.

CHAPTER 29

UNCLE CLARENCE

In Yan Yan Gurt:

On the surface, Uncle Clarence appeared to be a very different person to Maliyan. He was a bush farmer with a lifetime of demanding physical work behind him. He prided himself on his common sense, which Maliyan viewed as not infrequently a lack of education and tolerance more than sense. He was a fierce and loyal protector of his family, land, and sheep. Maliyan's more educated, broad-minded, deep-thinking and subtle alignment with the energetic world was at odds with Uncle Clarence and most bush folk of his generation.

Uncle Clarence's farmhouse was clean and tidy. The fortnightly visit from the subsidised aged care program made a noticeable impact. However, when Maliyan opened his fridge to get milk for a cup of tea, it looked as though it had not been cleaned since his tea-maker had gone down the hill (his wife had died and been buried in the cemetery at the bottom of the hill). The cleaners didn't do fridges, and he must have thought fridges were either self-cleaning or not worth the effort. The shelves were smeared with long-forgotten spills. Half-used jars with ancient use-by dates sported mouldy exteriors. It would have been rude to clean it, so she closed the door and remembered one of her uncle's sayings.

"I don't look at use-by dates. That's what we've got this for!" He would then point to his nose. "Besides, none of you kids ever died!"

He had a way of talking that made every sentence combative. Instead of saying, "I trust my sense of smell," he would stare at you accusingly, point to his nose and say, "That's what this is for," as if it were as plain as the dumb nose on your face. It was a way of saying, "I'm not stupid. You are!" That's why Maliyan always ignored his rather insulting conversational manner. She knew that it was insecurity. His underlying fears made him quick to attack and slow to apologise. Sometimes, when Maliyan was young and they would drive past the wealthier, larger farms, she would ask him, "Do we know them?" He would reply, "No, mate. Bloody oath. They don't talk to the likes of us." Maliyan never did accept the "us" that he was including her in.

They sat outside on the verandah in a patch of warming winter sun. Mornings and evenings in Yan Yan Gurt were as cold as The Flat, but the afternoons were considerably warmer.

"What have you been doing?" asked Maliyan.

Uncle Clarence shrugged and said, "Don't know anyone in Yan Yan Gurt anymore."

That wasn't exactly true, as he knew many families in the area. However, it was true that the town of a few hundred residents had changed significantly over the years. As he no longer had kids or wife to organise his social calendar, he didn't mix with the new town dwellers, and those he did know were becoming fewer and fewer. Besides that, towns, like people, go through stages.

When Maliyan was growing up, Yan Yan Gurt was a hive of community-minded farmers and families. The number of town residents remained the same over the years, but previously Yan Yan Gurt had a highly active community (in good part due to Uncle Clarence's wife). Everyone was involved in everything. "Everything" involved dances, fundraisers, town projects, the tennis club, the pony club, and many other heavily supported activities. However, the children of the town grew up and left for work and marriage, and Uncle Clarence's generation grew older. The next generation didn't take up the slack, and thus, the cycle of the tiny town went into a trough period.

CHAPTER 30

DEAD PEOPLE

"My big outing is to the cemetery," said Uncle Clarence. Maliyan wasn't sure if he was joking, but he wasn't. "There's nothing for me to do in town. Mrs Benson told me to come to church," he said with a roll of his eyes.

Town consisted of a railway station, two tiny, competing churches, a post office (which functioned a few times a week), a pub, several empty shops, a newly-launched and highly-anticipated general store with groceries, hamburgers, and milkshakes, and an occasionally open internet cafe with tea, sandwiches, and two basic computers, (which was ahead of its time when originally established by Uncle Clarence's wife).

"I can't even go down to the dam," said Uncle Clarence, "because it costs a damn $20 to get in. I was born down there. I should be allowed to get in for free!"

In the 1960s, the Burrendong Dam was built. As the dam filled, it flooded several historic areas. A section of country near Yan Yan Gurt, where Uncle Clarence was born, was one of them and became a pay-to-enter recreation park for skiers, fishers, boaters, and campers.

"So," said Uncle Clarence, "I go down to the cemetery and talk to all my mates."

Maliyan could imagine him walking between the graves of generations of relatives and mates—good exercise, memories, and connection. What did it matter if the connection was with spirits without bodies rather than spirits with bodies? In one sense, we are all "dead people" because we all live in spirit form, whether we have a physical body or not. Or, if you prefer, we are all alive.

CHAPTER 31

MICE AND MEN

A neighbouring farmer, a generation younger than Uncle Clarence, pulled up.

"G'day mate," he said. "Just callin' in to see how ya' goin'."

He nodded to Maliyan and then said of Uncle Clarence, "He shouldn't still be here. He's too old to be on a farm."

The neighbouring farmer had a herd of cattle and was planning to retire soon, as he was in his sixties. He wasn't a born-and-bred, three-generational farmer like Uncle Clarence. He moved from the city several decades ago and took pride in his ideas, which he frequently and uninvitedly shared with others.

He was fond of explaining, "I don't look at the weather forecast. I look around me. A few years back, they kept warning of a drought, but the Kurrajongs were flowering. My goats were all having twins, and the kangaroos had one joey on the ground and one, even younger, in the pouch. [Kangaroos can deliberately pause the development of a baby if conditions aren't favourable.] So I knew it would be alright. When it's going to be dry, the ants collect high moisture content food and take it back to their nests, and they weren't doing that."

His ideas weren't new. Many were based on the old under-standing of nature and animals "knowing" things ahead of time. What was different was that he didn't unconsciously feel these things in his bones as Uncle Clarence did; he actively sought to identify what they were and then explain them to other people. While he was surely annoying, he was a well-intended man and offered to help Uncle Clarence fix his broken tractor. Uncle Clarence needed the help, so he listened to his neighbour's mono-logues with an occasional, "Uh-huh."

"At least, the mice are gone," said the farmer as they all ambled towards the tractor. Turning to Maliyan, he explained, "In the plague, I put out lots of buckets of water. The buggers ran up the ramp, fell in the water, and drowned. You couldn't poison them because it would poison the dogs and the wildlife. Then, I put all the dead mice near the ant piles, and by the next day, they were gone."

"I see," said Maliyan screwing up her face.

Uncle Clarence was of the generation where the harsher reali-ties of farming life (mostly death) were kept from children and, to an extent, even from the women.

"You have to work in a seasonally appropriate way," lectured the farmer. "If it's too hot, some jobs have to wait till autumn."

"I just keep workin'," said Uncle Clarence under his breath. "Fruit won't wait. Sheep won't wait."

CHAPTER 32

SORRY AND SAD

After the tractor was fixed and the farmer left, Maliyan said, "I'll have to move into the shade. This sun has a bit of bite."

"Bite? It's bloody beautiful!" said Uncle Clarence. "You've lived in the south too long."

After a pause, he said, "I'll have to put the farm on the market soon. It's too lonely here on my own."

He had already sold nearly all of his tens of thousands of sheep and most of the land. The peach orchard had long ago been pulled out. Maliyan gazed at the packing shed below the house where the orchard once flourished. That shed was where she earned her first bit of money and learned a little about the value of hard work. Although the children were probably a blessing and a curse as packing shed staff, it was all hands on deck during the peak summer season. Uncle Clarence still owned the farmhouse, numerous sheds, the house paddocks, and a few sheep (his prize-winning ewe, a sheep with a disability, and a couple of stray sheep friends). Although he complained about his loneliness, he also said that if he lived in a town, he'd be dead in two weeks.

"You don't want to buy it, do you?" asked Uncle Clarence.

"It's my favourite place in the world," said Maliyan honestly, but shook her head. "Besides, we like it when *you* are here, not when you are not."

"I've made a lot of mistakes," he said quietly.

"No..." Maliyan started saying, but then stopped as she realised what he was doing. He had made many, it was true.

"Too many mistakes," he said with a shake of his head.

He didn't want to name those mistakes, but many of them, Maliyan already knew about. She let him be sad. Now was an excellent time to be sorry.

CHAPTER 33

SPARKLY BLUE

On the surface, Uncle Clarence appeared to be a very different person to Maliyan. However, as he aged and his fear of dying and regret of past mistakes took centre stage, the two seemed far more alike than they were different. Their DNA had somehow meshed and fused. Death collapses boundaries in a way that life never can.

Why do siblings differ as to which side of the family they will take after in appearance, psychic leanings, aspirations, connectedness, and belonging? A child may love both sides, but their physical and energetic DNA will align more closely with a particular strand running through their generational history.

Maliyan stared into Uncle Clarence's unusually sparkly blue eyes, encased by a seemingly inappropriate, un-sparkly, arthritic, almost ninety-year-old body, and the two of them were profoundly more connected than separated. The courage she saw in her uncle's eyes was also hers. It took her not into untamed bushland, but into untamed interior terrain. The same pair of sparkly blue eyes, Maliyan's and Uncle Clarence's, stared at each other and said goodbye, although sparkly blue eyes can never really say goodbye.

❦

THE NEXT DAY, MALIYAN BEGAN HER DRIVE BACK TO THE FLAT. She intended to stop somewhere overnight and didn't leave at the crack of dawn. However, synchronicity took control, and she decided to do the whole drive in one day.

At one point, she changed lanes on the freeway and saw that in the lane she had just exited, a large wooden ladder, which must have fallen off a truck, lay strewn across the road. An accident waiting to happen. Synchronicity made sure it didn't happen to her. Hopefully not anyone else either.

As she hadn't left early enough for a one-day drive, it was a race against the winter dusk. Winter won, and the last few hours were in the dark. However, fortuitously, it was full moon. As Maliyan cut across from the freeway to The Flat, crisscrossing the winding, unlit, narrow country roads, the full moon guided her and kept her company, so that she felt her home was not in the distance but with her the entire time.

UNKNOTTED

CHAPTER 34
SOLARA STARLING

In The Flat:

"Guess who's getting married?" Luna said a little smugly, one evening.

"No idea," replied Maliyan.

"Dr Tye!"

"Tye?" repeated Maliyan as she tried to process that information. "To who?"

"A woman from Byron Bay," explained Luna. "Her name is Solara Starling—well, I assume that's her adopted name."

He added with a grin, "Her name is probably Sue Smith."

Maliyan smiled and asked, "How do you know?"

"I saw Tye at the pool, and as he has been away all year, I asked him what's been happening?"

At the end of last year, Tye's mother suddenly died. She lived in a town about an hour north of the beach-blessed, wellness-soaked Byron Bay. Her town was a conservative retirement enclave, at least compared to the crystal shops and cafe culture of Byron Bay. At the time, Tye told Maliyan that he was going to take some time off to process the last few years ("the last few years" meaning the death of his son, his divorce, and now the death of his mother). He said he would most likely stay a while up north after the funeral. And that was the last Maliyan heard of him.

"And what *has* been happening?" asked Maliyan eagerly.

"A lot," said Luna with a wink. "He said that he was living at his mother's house while the probate was processing, and decided to go to a grief retreat in Byron Bay. Solara was the teacher/healer."

Luna put his hands up to indicate no more questions, and that was all he knew.

CHAPTER 35

HEALING THE HOLLOW

Maliyan decided it was time for a check-up and saw Dr Tye later that week.

"I bet your patients are very glad to have you back," said Maliyan.

Tye smiled humbly and said, "Luna told you my news?"

"Of course," said Maliyan, giving him a hug. "I couldn't be more thrilled for you."

"Thank you," said Tye. "And I hear that Luna is with you these days?"

"As cohabiters," corrected Maliyan. "Not couplers."

"I see," said Tye, who was sure that he wasn't sure about their relationship at all.

Tye then told Maliyan his story. He went to his mother's funeral feeling nothing because he didn't have the space to feel any more loss.

"Living in her home was like living in a tomb," said Tye. "Death and loss and memories haunted me day and night, but for some reason, I couldn't leave. Something in me knew that if I left, I'd be taking the death with me like a shadow. After a few weeks of utter misery, I saw an ad for a grief retreat in Byron Bay. It was called

Healing the Hollow. As you know, I am by nature a conservative person, but when you hit rock bottom, there's nothing left to lose. Indeed, the retreat began with the words, 'In the fall, may we find our footing.'"

"Tell me about Solara," said Maliyan.

Tye laughed and said, "At first, I thought she was just weird, and I wondered what I had got myself into. But I didn't want to go back to my tomb, so I stuck out the two-week retreat, which was similarly painful to my tomb, but at least there was some chance of... something."

"Hope," offered Maliyan. "Healing."

"Yes," said Tye. "We are very different, but somehow we help each other. I ground her."

He added with a smile, "She probably thinks I weigh her down."

He turned his gaze to the world beyond the window pane, the passing people on the street. When Maliyan first met Tye last year, before she was aware of his personal problems, he cryptically commented about that same window that it was like living in a fishbowl. It no longer seemed fishy in the slightest.

He continued, "And she shows me that life is not what I thought."

CHAPTER 36

HAVING OURSELVES

That evening:

"I'm glad that Tye has someone now," said Luna. "It was sad that he and Leteisha broke up, seeing as they were both good people and got along well. It seemed like pointless pain."

"Being good and getting along are not the markers for staying together," said Maliyan, "and every pain has a point, but I understand what you are saying."

"What are the markers for staying together then?" asked Luna.

"Why should staying together be the goal?" said Maliyan.

"What is the point of getting married then?" said Luna.

ON SHAKANA:

Maliyan recalled that on Shakana, no one got married. Marriage was seen as a social convention for planets like Earth. On Shakana, everyone felt deeply connected to everyone, as well as to nature and the very essence of existence. There was no need or desire to seek out special arrangements. Nevertheless, everyone's life path did involve specific people and situations, and that was respected as invaluable for each person's life path.

"Often, we cannot see the pattern of someone's connection to us until the end of our lives," said Shunyata. "We look back and see our paths intertwining over the years and understand the way our matrices were conjoined."

Another time, Shunyata said, "Love is eternal when it is unconditional, but interpersonal arrangements can change, for many reasons. Sometimes, those changes can be mitigated by learning certain lessons. Sometimes, they cannot be. Nevertheless, how a person responds to the changes is always within their realm of power."

ॐ

"What **is** the point of getting married?" replied Maliyan.

"I guess," said Luna, "it can feel comforting to know that someone will be there through thick and thin, even if you act badly, that they're not going to disappear."

Maliyan laughed and said, "If people act badly, isn't it better that they learn not to? Being left is a primary way people learn to behave better."

"True," said Luna.

"Anyway, given that you, *personally,* have such a high propensity towards independence," said Maliyan, "you, *personally*, would easily feel trapped."

After a pause, Luna said, "I think the best solution is for people to wake up every morning and know they are not trapped and neither is the other person, each person can freely choose to be there or not, it is up to each one to make it work, and if someone wants to leave, both people will be fine because, after all, we only ever have ourselves anyway."

"Instead of tying the knot," said Maliyan, "it would serve us all better to practice being unknotted beings."

ORDERING THE DISORDER

CHAPTER 37

BRAIN AND BODY

Three years ago, when Maliyan was living in Nanima, she had a long-term back problem. Eventually, she had surgery for it, which didn't directly fix the issue, but it seemed to go away anyway. Strangely, since starting her healing practice in The Flat, the problem returned with a vengeance and transformed into a neurological functioning problem on the whole right side of her body. It was strange because one would think that when involved in healing work, one would reap the benefits of it oneself.

The neurological issue was the main reason for Maliyan's visit to Dr Tye. As it involved loss of function and shakiness, Tye naturally wanted to send her for scans for all the neurological conditions that affect people over fifty, like Alzheimer's, Parkinson's, dementia, stroke, MS, autoimmune issues, and various other assorted and fun diseases. Although, of course, people should do whatever is helpful and appropriate to them individually, Maliyan didn't want to go for the tests.

"The thing is," she said, "if you don't mind me being blunt [these days, Tye was far more used to blunt because of Solara], I'm not doing that. I don't like medical tests. They incite fear, and fear feeds disease. If I thought it was necessary, I would go, but I have self-diagnosed myself with FND [Functional Neurological Disorder is a malfunction between brain and body for no apparent reason]. They'll make me go through all the tests with their inadvertent fear-mongering mentality, then they'll say there is nothing wrong with me. Then, I'll tell them that I think it's FND, which many specialists know little about. Then, they'll send me to a movement therapist to learn movements that I am already aware of. And they'll tell me to go to a psychologist. Tye, I can run rings around any psychologist. I'll end up saying something rude."

Tye laughed and said, "Okay, okay. How about this? Go to the chiropractor. That'll clear the nerve pathways and help you to get better brain/body communication."

"Great idea," said Maliyan.

And she did.

CHAPTER 38

EXPERIENCING EXPERIENCES

I*n Shakana:*

"Could you make my FND go away?" asked Maliyan.

"I could," said Shunyata, "but what would be the point of that?"

"I would feel better."

"Did you go to Earth to 'feel better'?"

Maliyan didn't answer that, so Shunyata continued, "Please remember that your consciousness is not in your body. Your body is in your consciousness. Your true state is that of an expansive spirit, but you chose to have an Earth adventure. A part of your spirit solidified into the construct of your body. When you die, you expand out again to your full-dimensional energetic self. But, for now, you are experiencing the experiences that you wanted to experience for your own purposes."

"What purposes?"

"Growth," said Shunyata. "Like everyone else, you shrank your being into physical form and then got amnesia about who you really are."

"Why would anyone choose to forget such a thing?" asked Maliyan.

261

"By diving deeply into forgetfulness, you get to experience the abandon and glory of waking up. It's exhilarating!"

Feeling quite unexhilarated, Maliyan said, "I'm trying to reconstruct my body—in my sleep, in meditations and healing—but it isn't working."

"You assume that something is wrong," said Shunyata.

"Hmmm, I would prefer it to go away."

"Let it be what it is. It is there for a reason. Allow it to be that. That is all I can tell you for now, but you are being given all the help you need."

With that, she disappeared, and Malayan woke from her half-meditative, half-dream state.

CHAPTER 39

SIGNAL NOT SEEKER

On Geboor:

It was a wild, windy, wintery day—perfect for keeping tourists away from the top of Geboor. Maliyan walked its blistery, blowy tracks and went deeper into the towering trees, which were bending and barking in the wind.

Eventually, a voice spoke to her—not out loud, but inwardly, telepathically. Telepathy is not reading someone else's mind. It's a willingness to be on the same wavelength as another person or being. It's picking up on the thought vibrations of the shared territory. People in love do it all the time, and often finish each other's sentences, know what the other is feeling, and mirror their beloved's mind. There are many ways to be in love. If you are in one of them, you will become available to someone else's vibrational frequency.

"My name is Cernunnos," said a voice which seemed to be speaking through the wind and trees. "I am the winter spirit, an elemental. Or, if you prefer, an archetype of regenerative power. In return, for your presence here today, how may I assist you?"

"Can you help me understand the FND I am experiencing?" said Maliyan.

Feeling that that may seem selfish or small-minded when talking to a grand elemental, she added, "If that's okay, I mean..."

Somehow, that seemed even more pathetic. The wind picked up and roared in all directions as if the elemental was scanning her body.

"The FND is not a malfunction, but a recalibration. It is a dismantling of old energetic architecture to make room for a new operating system. Your body is adjusting to a higher vibrational bandwidth. The old pathways of energy, nervous response, and habitual motion are being rewired, and the disruption is part of the upgrade process. Just as a computer can freeze while installing an important update, your body can temporarily lose normal function as it integrates the energetic shift. It isn't dysfunction, it's transmutation. It is the disintegration of an old definition of self that is no longer congruent with your frequency. You are operating at a higher vibration, but remnants of the old identity linger in the physical habits of the body. Your body is resisting the frequency mismatch. The tension must express itself—either emotionally, situationally, or physically—until full alignment is achieved."

After a fertile pause, Cernunnos continued, "The right side of your body is a representation of past templates. As you ascend into a new template of being, a more enlightened state, your right side is dropping the weight of outdated structures. The dysfunction is a refusal to carry the old codes forward. You cannot continue into the next version of reality with the old patterns embedded in your physical matrix. Your nervous system is your interface—both with physical reality and with subtler frequencies. You are clearing static, creating space in the nervous system, and disabling pathways that are no longer relevant to your soul's next steps. Your system is recalibrating to emit higher frequencies, much like a tuning fork."

Maliyan jumped nervously as the trees creaked and cracked loudly under the weight of the wind.

Cernunnos continued, "I came to this mountain to talk to the spirit of Geboor, and I must go now, but remember, there is nothing wrong with you. You are rewiring and shedding timelines.

Don't resist the process. It's a coded message from your future self, saying, 'You're ready for more.'

> *You are not a seeker.*
> *You are a signal.*
>
> *You are not a space holder.*
> *You are a carrier of frequency.*
>
> *You are not inviting the light.*
> *You are the light."*

The wind momentarily stopped shrieking, the trees stood still, and Cernunnos was gone.

SPIRIT OF SPRING

CHAPTER 40

HOUSE AND HEART

Six weeks later, in early spring:

Although the mornings were still cold in The Flat and mist lingered in the creek hollows beneath Maliyan's home, the late morning spring sunshine breathed warmth into the bones of the town. As Maliyan walked to the shops, golden wattle pompoms spilled over the footpaths. Emerging daffodils and jonquils cheered quickening gardens. Magpies sang from fence posts with boldness, and rainbow-coloured rosellas flitted between the gum branches. The previously empty outside tables of Paperboy were now full and flourishing.

Approaching the cafe, Maliyan watched Luna talk to his customers. A trendy city couple with their adult offspring engaged Luna in a bright conversation.

"This honey is divine," said the woman with excessive gesticulation. "Where did you get it?"

Luna shrugged and said, "I don't know, hun, it's probably the cheapest honey I could get."

"Oh," said the woman awkwardly, not being able to think of anything fast enough to rescue her faux pas.

Maliyan smiled at Luna's lack of concern about the woman's pretensions. He began scribbling the orders of some of the shady gay guys.

"Hi, babes," said Luna. "How are we all today?"

"How's your house hunting going?" asked one of them.

"Slowly," replied Luna. "The ones I like are all acreages. Too expensive."

Seeing Maliyan behind Luna, one of them said, "Your housemate is here."

Luna turned to face Maliyan, smiled, turned back to his friends and said, "She's not my housemate, boo. She's my *heart*-mate."

⁂

THAT EVENING:

"It's a bit lonely house hunting on my own," said Luna. "Don't you ever get lonely?"

"No, darling," said Maliyan. "I never feel lonely."

"Oh," said Luna.

Feeling that she had missed a cue, Maliyan asked, "Why?"

"No reason," said Luna, as he went to his room.

⁂

THE NEXT MORNING:

"People like me don't feel lonely," said Maliyan, "because we see things everywhere that other people don't see. It's too busy to feel alone."

Luna didn't want to talk about all the invisible things he couldn't see that apparently kept Maliyan in constant company.

"However, not having the capacity to feel alone," said Maliyan softly, "doesn't mean that I don't enjoy people."

Luna huffed in a dissatisfied way, but kept listening.

"Luna," said Maliyan, "you mean the world to me."

Now, he smiled. Broadly, authentically, emotionally.

"Have a great day," he said as he grabbed his keys. "See you tonight, heart-mate."

CHAPTER 41

THE ROAD REMEMBERS

Luna watched the little spring lambs dotted across the paddock. Some were curled up close to their mothers, while others wobbled around on skinny legs, unsure but determined. They were pure white, unlike their mothers, who had dirtier wool. A few jumped and kicked in short bursts, full of energy that they didn't know what to do with. The mothers kept a quiet eye on them, heads down as they grazed, occasionally calling out with a soft bleat. The lambs didn't stray far—always circling back to press into their mothers' bellies.

"It's so peaceful," Luna said to Iggy in the passenger seat, who was also fascinated by the lambs. "And so...new."

They were driving down Station Road, a dirt track not far from The Flat. It led to a now-defunct railway station. The road wound past about fifteen farmsteads. Luna had been to inspect a house that was originally a farmhand's cottage, now on a subdivided five acres. The farm that it once belonged to still operated as a sheep property. Its shearing shed was not far from the farmhand's house.

Further down the road, a middle-aged couple, both on their mobile phones, waved to Luna's passing car.

"Bad phone reception," Luna said to Iggy. "They probably have to stand outside to make calls. Maybe, they think we belong to one of the farms—someone's son or uncle or friend. Not many people would drive down this road."

Old dirt roads have their own tracks worn into them. You have to get to know them and follow the flow of the road, navigating around potholes and avoiding corrugations. If you insist on driving in a straight line, it doesn't work. You have to allow the worn tracks of the road, made from the coming and goings of the farmers, to lead the way. You have to let the road drive you. The road remembers the way.

We may think that if our path in life is not a smooth, upward trajectory, then something is wrong or, at least, it's time inefficient. But if the winding, sometimes erratic, road—the one full of dips and detours—is the one for us, then it will be the most direct route because the smooth one will end up throwing many blocks at us. We often expect progress to look like a clean, upward line, but life generally charts a zigzag course, full of peaks and valleys. The winding path will carry us faster and deeper than the straight one, when it is ours to take.

CHAPTER 42

WATCHER'S HOUR

week later:

It was 3:00 a.m.—the psychic hour, the watcher's hour —when the veil between the worlds is thin, the soul whispers in the dark, and the inter-dimensional gate swings wide open. Strange visions drift through the mind, magnetically reorienting consciousness toward other realms.

"You will not hear from me for a while," said Shunyata.

"Why?" asked Maliyan. "I need you."

"You will still have our help," said Shunyata. "We never leave you. But you need to concentrate on other things for a while."

Maliyan remembered that the Wise Ones often said, *"It is not we who leave you, but you who leave us."*

"Everything we have given you is inside you," continued Shunyata, "and we leave you with this last reminder:

1. You are who you are meant to be, and that is enough.
2. Your life is yours to live as you choose.
3. Freedom is your birthright.
4. You are an eternal, timeless being.
5. You are endlessly loved and supported by creation.
6. Time is an illusion. There is only now.
7. Trust the perfect timing of your life. It knows the way.
8. Your needs will always be met.
9. When you insist, you create resistance.
10. You are a channel for love, happiness, and healing.

Practice these principles in all the big and little ways, and we will see you on the other side.

HEART OF HOME

CHAPTER 43

FENCE LINE

Luna and Maliyan walked the boundary fence of the five-acre property Luna had recently inspected. The spring afternoon breathed expectantly around them. The nearby ranges stretched behind—soft ridges, rounded hills, and the peak of Geboor. A breeze carried the scent of wattle and grass. The property was mostly cleared, with scattered gums offering dappled shade. The neighbour's dam shimmered in the light. It was peaceful, but also pregnant.

"The other morning, you said that I mean the world to you," said Luna.

"Yes?" said Maliyan.

"I know that you love me," continued Luna, "but you don't really need me... or anyone."

His words drifted out across the paddock, stolen by the mischievous breeze.

"You are my *link to life*," said Maliyan.

Although Luna didn't understand what Maliyan meant exactly, she said it so definitely that his question seemed to disappear.

"So what do you think?" asked Luna.

They leaned on the wire fence, looking across the paddock. Several ewes grazed near the dam, their lambs close by.

"Gorgeous," said Maliyan.

"The house," scolded Luna.

"Very fixable. Cute and comfortable. What more could you want?"

Luna nodded.

"We can be honest with each other, right?" he said.

"Of course, love. If we're not honest with each other, then who are we even in a relationship with? Not the real us."

He nodded again, slower this time. "Right."

A magpie called from a nearby gum. Several lambs sprang at invisible things, all legs and enthusiasm, their mothers barely glancing up.

"Would you..." asked Luna falteringly. "Be interested in buying it with me?"

"Because it's too much for you... on your own?" questioned Maliyan.

Luna nodded.

"And... we'd be housemates?" Maliyan asked.

"*Heart*-mates," corrected Luna quickly.

"Heart-mates," Maliyan repeated. "Yes, you are my heart-mate."

"I know you don't worry about money," continued Luna, "But I do. And I don't want either of us to get stuck in something we can't manage."

"Yes?"

"So... I had an idea."

"Uh-huh."

"What about a *five-year plan*?" proposed Luna. "It wouldn't mean we have to stay five years if something really important happened, but it would give us both a safety net. We'd do our best to make it work—for the sake of the property... and each other. After five years, we could reassess and, if necessary, sell the house and move on—none the worse."

"None the worse..." repeated Maliyan.

CHAPTER 44

THE WINTER SPIRIT

On Geboor:

Now that the weather had turned for the better, the summit of Geboor was drawing its usual gaggle of day-trippers. Maliyan watched them from a distance—tourists of all kinds, from all places, chatting loudly in their home languages, taking cheesy-smiley selfies and moving on, as if the point was simply to tick off another destination rather than actually *be* in one. No one noticed the stillness of the gums, the blue above, or the way the light bounced across the granite boulders.

Fortunately, it wasn't hard to get away from them. They were intent on following the trodden main path. Maliyan took a small track worn by wallabies and solitary seekers. The sound of tourists dropped away. The gums stood tall and still, their trunks pale and peeling, their new leaves a tender green. The wind had softened since winter, though it still held a crisp edge.

She could see the little town of Black Forest below. Nowadays, almost everyone drove up the mountain. But in days gone by, many locals would have walked. She thought about the farmers' children, with cousins in tow, climbing the lower slopes without a second thought—chasing one another through the bush, playing in the gullies, laughing at their silly jokes, never wondering if they belonged there. Of course, they belonged. They belonged so completely that the idea of not belonging never entered their minds.

A sudden breath of cold air brushed the back of Maliyan's neck. It wasn't just the wind that was surprising. It was something else. A different presence.

Cernunnos—the Winter Spirit.

Why was he here now? The cold gathered around her, intentional and focused—a gateway of sorts.

"My time is done," said Cernunnos. "But I am here to honour the turning, to hand over the season, to mark the threshold between what had been and what is now."

"Are you sad your time is over?" asked Maliyan, although even as the thought formed, she knew it was a foolish question. Grand spirits like Cernunnos don't trifle with the tremblings of human emotion. He was an archetype of strength and independence.

She felt a shift in the air currents, a flick of movement through the trees, some leaves skittering in a small spiral across her feet.

A flippant laugh from the Winter Spirit.

"I do not return from sentiment," said Cernunnos, "but from ancient rhythm—just long enough to pass on the thread of guardianship."

Maliyan's thoughts returned to Luna's proposal yesterday. They needed to make a decision today so that an offer could be made. That's why Maliyan was on Geboor. To listen.

Not explaining the details of what she was talking about— details she presumed Cernunnos would sense—Maliyan said,

"If I say yes, what happens if it falls apart?"

Cernunnos said nothing.

"What happens if it doesn't?" asked Maliyan.

The sun reflected off a shiny roof below in Black Forest and sent a white beam towards Geboor.

"I understand Luna's fears," she continued. "But I have my own. Different ones. I think."

Cernunnos was still silent.

Maliyan remembered that on Shakana, no one insisted that relationships declare themselves and fit neatly into names and categories. They would not do the disservice to one another of insisting a relationship must be a certain way, for a certain duration, with specific obligations or societal formats.

Almost all beings there lived their connections without fixed names—partnerships of soul, not form. They saw it as a distortion to bind one another to roles or timelines for the comfort of certainty.

They surrendered to the deeper intelligence of Creation's timing—the sacred rhythm that draws people together when the resonance is right, and allows them to part if and when their shared purpose is fulfilled. Although really, it was understood that there could be no true parting.

They let synchronicity guide how their connections began, how long they remained, and when they were ready to evolve or end. Synchronicity carried the blueprint of every meeting: the teaching, the timing, the transformation.

It saw far beyond what the personal mind could grasp, and because of this, they trusted it completely. Whether joy or grief, growth or stillness, synchronicity understood the invisible work being done between people.

Shunyata would sometimes remind Maliyan that the true nature of a relationship was generally not seen in the midst of it. On Shakana, it was often at the end of one's life—when the wide arc of time curved into a quiet overview—that the shape of each connection became clear. The meanings came into focus. What seemed random was revealed as precise. What felt fleeting was seen as complete. Until then, relationships were lived not as defined paths, but as *open, fluid, unlabelled presence.*

❧

"WHAT IF HE HURTS ME?" ASKED MALIYAN. "WORSE, WHAT IF I hurt him?"

"What if he blooms?" said the Winter Spirit.

With the thought of blooming, Cernunnos transmitted the following final words and receded into the realms from which he came.

I am bound to nothing.
Yet, I belong to all.

When the world turns,
I turn too.

I do not cling,
but nor do I drift.

I meet each season with gusto,
and then I say *fare well*.

I do not ask the ice to stay,
nor mourn the thaw of frost.

What falls, falls.
What blooms, blooms.
I offer myself to each in turn.

I carry many a promise,
but I never break vows—
for I am wholly present to what is.

I honour your silence.
I honour your voice.
I honour your yes.
I honour your no.

CHAPTER 45

TOURMALINE THREAD

Maliyan pulled up at home, having just returned from Geboor. Ribbons of mauve and rose flooded the dusk sky. The fading light wrapped the paddock and creek below her house in its final statement of the day.

Luna sat cross-legged on the lounge room floor, unusually still. He didn't look up when Maliyan entered. Something was resting in his lap.

Still silent, Luna passed her a small box.

Maliyan looked surprised. Luna was not one to give presents. He barely tolerated receiving them—responding with an uncomfortable, objecting gratitude, as if the gift would saddle him with an eternal obligation to return the favour someday. He had certainly never given Maliyan a gift before.

Inside the box was a necklace, understated in its simple beauty. A fine silver chain with a polished piece of watermelon tourmaline. Rose-pink at the centre, melting into forest-green at the edges—perfectly balanced.

"I know you don't wear jewellery," said Luna.

It was true. She didn't. But she hadn't realised he'd noticed that. She liked the *idea* of jewellery, but every time she wore it, something felt... constricted. As if the object was blocking the flow of energy out from her body. She always ended up taking it off again after a few hours.

"But I had it made anyway," shrugged Luna.

"I love it," said Maliyan.

"It's the watermelon tourmaline you gave me at the end of summer when I was obsessing over something or other," said Luna.

Maliyan recalled Luna's *watermelon-special* obsession at Paperboy. The original crystal came in a box that said,

Watermelon tourmaline will help you connect with your feelings. It will soften the emotional space around you and bring closeness to your relationships.

"It changed form," said Luna, picking up the necklace and holding it to the light, "but it's the same crystal of an idea."

Maliyan smiled approvingly.

"You've given it to me before we've made our final decision on the property," said Maliyan.

"On the rare occasion I give a gift," winked Luna, "it's unconditional."

"Well then," said Maliyan, "let's see what we can make of this property in five years."

"Yes, let's see," said Luna with a calm smile. "*And* let's see what we can make of *ourselves.*"

The End

SUMMARY OF NANIMA SERIES

A contemplative journey of **spiritual evolution, soulful relationships, and the quiet healing power of nature.**

Spanning four deeply personal and spiritually rich books—**Nanima, Geboor, Sonder**, and **The Flat**—this series follows Maliyan, an insightful and grounded seeker whose path unfolds across the quiet towns and wild landscapes of rural Australia.

Through shifting relationships, ancestral stirrings, and encounters with both seen and unseen guides, Maliyan's life becomes a mirror for our own inner transformation. Alongside her are Luna—intuitive, witty, and playfully avoidant as he learns to love truly—and Bell-Bell, whose brilliance and volatility reflect the challenges of change and the yearning for wholeness.

The *Nanima Series* offers not just a story, but a spiritual companion. It invites you to walk the path of growth gently, to listen deeply to the land and your own spirit, and to remember that evolution is both quiet and profound.

ABOUT THE AUTHOR

On top of Mount Macedon (Aboriginal name is Geboor) overlooking the small rural town of Woodend, Australia (Black Forest in the Nanima Series).

Donna Goddard is a spiritual author whose work blends clarity, devotion, and metaphysical insight. With more than twenty published books across spiritual nonfiction, fiction, poetry, and children's literature, she writes to uplift consciousness and offer healing through words.

Donna's Facebook author page has over 400,000 followers from around the world, and her YouTube channel has received more than three million views. Her books are read by spiritual seekers globally and are known for their honesty, poetic style, and transformative energy.

Her writing is an offering—to help others awaken their own inner spirit, trust its guidance, and create a life of depth, beauty, and quiet joy.

All links at https://linktr.ee/donnagoddard

RATINGS AND REVIEWS

Donna would be most grateful for any ratings or reviews.

Fiction
Waldmeer Series: A Spiritual Fiction Series
Nanima Series: Spiritual Fiction
Riverland Series (children's fiction 6 to 9 years)
The Fox Tales (children's fiction 8 to 12 years)

Nonfiction
Love and Devotion Series
Sweet Spirit Series
Dance: A Spiritual Affair
Writing: A Spiritual Voice
Strange Words: Poems and Prayers
Love's Longing
Master of Me: Meditations

www.ingramcontent.com/pod-product-compliance
Lightning Source LLC
Chambersburg PA
CBHW030612170726
48283CB00002B/568